Inspector's Holiday

Inspector's Holiday

An Inspector Heimrich Mystery

RICHARD LOCKRIDGE

J. B. Lippincott Company
Philadelphia & New York

Copyright © 1971 by Richard Lockridge

First Edition

Printed in the United States of America
Library of Congress Catalog Card Number: 79–134933

For Hildy

1

It was not snowing on the morning of that thirtieth of March. Heimrich had gloomily supposed it would be; had envisioned a blizzard. But at seven-thirty in the morning the low house on a hill overlooking the Hudson merely shook a little in the northwest wind. The wind raced clouds across a sky which, at intervals, showed blue. The temperature was even a degree or two above freezing. The northwest wind would change that. Falling into the twenties by afternoon; probability of occasional snow flurries. They would be away by then.

Heimrich put his electric razor in its case and the case in the space measured for it in a small, square suitcase. He closed the case. He made sure that the tag was on it. He carried it out to the living room and put it with the others by the door. There were a good many of the others, and the tags were on all of them.

Susan was sitting by the fireplace, in which no fire was burning. The house was warm enough, but she was wearing her heavy winter coat. Merton Heimrich did not say anything. He did not even lift his eyebrows.

7

"I'm fine, dear," Susan said. "Just fine. I—I just put my coat on to be ready when he gets here."

She didn't look fine, Heimrich thought. She was always slender; she was thin now. Her face was thin, and there was little color in it. Heimrich walked across the room and stood and looked down at her.

"Just fine," Susan said. "Really, darling."

He kept on looking down at her.

She smiled at him. The smile was her own smile. A few weeks ago it had not been. It had been faint on her lips. Her lips were faint still under lipstick.

"Sure you are," Merton Heimrich told his wife, and sat down in a chair by hers and poured himself coffee. He drank from his cup. He said, "Sure you are." He got what conviction he could into his voice. He knew he hadn't got enough into it, and she reached across the table between them and put her hand on his. She said, "You make too much of things, darling. Really you do. Really I'm fine. It was just the flu. The flu everybody had."

"Sure," Heimrich said, and turned his hand over so he could press it on hers. "Just the flu everybody had."

Not everybody had had the flu that winter. Merton Heimrich, Inspector, New York State Police, had not had it. But Michael Faye had had it, mildly, and so had scores in the hamlet of Van Brunt, County of Putnam, State of New York. It had been that kind of a winter east of the Hudson. The first snow had come before Thanksgiving. Since it had fallen, nobody had seen bare ground. The state plows had left snow ranges on the sides of highways; the town road from which the Heimrichs' steep driveway climbs had been, at best, patchy with ice and rumpled snow, with sand strewn haphazardly on the steepest slopes. For three days at one time and two at another, Merton Heimrich had been snowed away from his office at the headquarters of Troop K, which is some miles south of Van Brunt.

Nobody could remember a winter such as this winter had been and, for that matter, still was being. Susan Heimrich had grown up in Van Brunt and could remember no such winter. Merton Heimrich, who had lived in Van Brunt since its firehouse had burned down and a charred body had been found in its ruins, could remember no winter which approached this winter in sheer malevolence. And a good many people had got the flu and a few had died of it.

Susan's flu had not, however she now insisted, been "just the flu that everybody had." There had been complications; eventually, there had been pneumonia. For most of February she had been in a hospital; once home, she had convalesced with, Merton thought, agonizing slowness. "I'm much better today," she had said, over and over, seeing anxiety in his face. "I'm much, much better." And the doctor had agreed that she was doing as well as could be expected, adding, with the understandable bitterness of a man who had to be much out in it, "In this kind of weather."

"She's let herself get run down," Dr. Forbes had said. "Fighting her way down every day to that shop of hers. Fighting her way home again. And worrying about you, come to that. Half the time out half the nights."

"The kind of job I've got," Heimrich had said to that. "A bit like the kind you've got, Doctor. People get sick at inconvenient times. They also kill at inconvenient times."

He had been told to make her rest more. Forbes had added, "What you really ought to do is get her away somewhere the weather's decent. It won't be, here, for God knows when. That's what you ought to do."

"Pretty hard to manage," Heimrich had told Dr. Forbes, who had merely shrugged his shoulders.

But, once thought about, it had not really been too hard to manage. He had accumulated leave and, as an inspector, could take it pretty much when he chose. There'd be a deep hole dug in the bank account. (But her face is so very thin; she

9

moves as if she were so very tired.) Young Michael was a freshman at Dartmouth, where the winter had probably been even worse. ("Dear Mother and Dad: They say it was fifty below at six o'clock this morning. We froze our way to breakfast. I got a midterm A in—")

Colonel, who is a moderately enormous Great Dane, and Mite, a solidly black tomcat who has somewhat absurdly outgrown his name, could stay at the vet's. They would not approve. Colonel, who is morose at best, would be disheartened to the point of collapse. If Mite could stay in his pen with him? "In Colonel's mind, Mite is his cat. In Colonel's mind, he invented Mite."

The veterinarian had looked his doubt. There was a place for boarding cats and a place for dogs, and each stayed in his proper place. But—well, they could try it. And Mrs. Heimrich certainly ought to get away. She'd had a tough time of it, from what he heard.

The shop was not a problem. Even in better winters, there is no rush of trade to the shop on Van Brunt Avenue, which is also NY 11F, with "susan faye, fabrics" lettered in italics on its front window. In most winters those who can afford to pay for Faye designs flee the country for city apartments. The more rugged permanents do not redecorate their big houses. Not even the most sanguine encourage themselves to drive miles on twisting, narrow roads, uphill and downhill through snow, to buy curtain fabrics. But until this year, Susan Heimrich, who had been Susan Faye before and after the death of Michael Faye, Sr., in Korea, had kept the shop open. Seldom interrupted by customers, she had stood in the back room of the shop and splashed bright colors. Some of her best designs had grown in mind and hand on winter days.

But this year she had closed the shop in late January because the road to it was so often hazardous and because, although she was really "fine," she had not felt up to working. The most vivid poster paints became dim to her eyes. She did not give up easily. Only when Merton Heimrich drove her to the doctor's office and they learned that the dimness of color, and the general shakiness of body, were among the results of a fever of a hundred and three did she admit to herself, or to anybody, that she wasn't "fine." And in the hospital, when the fever rose and breathing, even in an oxygen tent, was a gasping thing, her right hand still fluttered as if it held a brush.

The Snell Travel Service in Cold Harbor, which lies a few miles north of the hamlet of Van Brunt, thought first of the Caribbean. Such lovely weather there; the islands so exquisitely tropical in scenery and in weather; the beaches so magnificent, the life so gay. The Bahamas? The Virgin Islands? Jamaica would be wonderful. If, of course, they wanted to go farther? Get really off the beaten track? Some people she knew went every winter to the Costa del Sol on the Mediterranean in Spain. So unspoiled, they said it was. And the state-owned hotels, called *paradores*. Really splendid places, from what she'd heard.

Miss Gertrude Snell, who was Snell Travel Services, had not herself been to the Costa del Sol. But she had heard it was lovely. So foreign, but with English widely spoken. They could fly from Kennedy International to Madrid and from Madrid down to—"wait till I look it up"—Málaga and hire a car and drive along the coast—"unspoiled fishing villages all along the coast" she understood there were—until they found just the place they liked. It would be warm this time of year. Not perhaps as warm as, say, Jamaica. But certainly warmer than it was here. *Br-r-r!*

Heimrich's job sometimes requires flying in airplanes. He does not like them. He does not like long waits at airports for departures or long circling above airports for arrivals; he does not like the tedious distances airports are from places one wants to be. And Susan begins to quiver when airplane doors close with the awful finality of airplane doors. A ship?

Miss Snell believed there were ships. Merton Heimrich

11

thought she spoke as if she had for the first time heard of them. She could look it up. Of course, the weather would be perfect this time of year in Nassau, and there were such lovely hotels. But she would certainly look up the matter of ships. She would give Inspector Heimrich a ring.

It took her only a day to discover that one of man's first means of getting from one place to another was still available. There really was a ship. It went, of all places, to Málaga. "Which is quite near Gibraltar, actually. Only in Spain." And there was a sailing from New York on the thirtieth of March. Of course, it would take much longer than by plane. The ship —the S.S. *Italia* of the Italian Line, the ship was—was due in Málaga on April sixth. If Inspector and Mrs. Heimrich didn't mind so long a voyage—the ship took the southern route, of course, so the weather should be quite pleasant—she thought she could get a booking. First class? Although cabin was supposed to be very comfortable on the *Italia*. Not that the *Italia* was the *Michelangelo* or the *Raffaello*. She didn't say it was. But a very fine ship and only a little smaller than the line's two big ones and with stabilizers, so it shouldn't be a rough voyage at all, particularly on the southern route.

They talked it over. Susan said they didn't need to do it, because she was fine—getting stronger every day. And it would cost a lot. And if they waited, spring would come up to them. And if they went first class, Merton probably would have to take a dinner jacket. And—

But her eyes were brighter than he had seen them in many weeks. There was even something of the old gaiety in her voice. But of course they shouldn't—and what would they do with the animals? And—

Cabin 82, starboard side, on the S.S. *Italia,* sailing from the foot of West Fiftieth Street at noon on March 30. A check. rather sizable, exchanged for tickets and tags to go on suitcases; passports checked and found in good order; vaccination certificates provided by Dr. Forbes.

So they waited in the living room of the house on a hilltop from which they could look down on the Hudson River—currently full of ice—for a trooper to come in a police car to drive them in their own Buick to the city and the foot of West Fiftieth Street and the S.S. *Italia* of the Italian Line. They were due aboard not later than ten, and it was—Heimrich looked at his watch. It was ten minutes of eight. Any time, now. With the roads the way they were—

A car sounded at them from outside. Made it up the drive all right. (There was an icy stretch on which Heimrich himself had spun wheels the night before. He had spread on it the granulated clay which was used in Mite's toilet pan, and which works better than sand on icy spots.)

Heimrich went to the door and opened it, and the wind banged at him. But he is a big, solid man—he is inclined to think of himself as resembling a hippopotamus—and defeated the wind.

The man getting out of the unmarked sedan, with only its long radio antenna to identify it as a police car, was not the expected trooper. Lieutenant Charles Forniss of the State Police got out of the car and said, "Morning, M.L.," and came toward Heimrich. Heimrich said, "Hi, Charley," to the man who had worked with him for many years and hadn't had to come to drive them in. The day before at the barracks Forniss had said, "Take care of yourself. And take care of Susan." They had shaken hands and that was the good-by for the month or six weeks. Forniss hadn't come to act as chauffeur because he had to. He had come because he wanted to. Heimrich was not surprised; at least he was not very surprised. He was, on the other hand, very pleased. Forniss hadn't got up early for an inspector. He had got up early for a friend.

The two big men loaded suitcases into the police car. This was not particularly legal. The car was not for private use. But legality can be stretched. Coming back, Forniss would not have to drive up from the barracks to exchange the Heimrich Buick for the police car. He mentioned this. They stowed luggage in the trunk, and there seemed to be a good deal of it. Taking dinner clothes adds to luggage. ("We could just as well have gone cabin," Susan had said as they packed. "You can easily mail your dinner things back after you get off the ship," Miss Snell had said, with the confidence of one who had never tried it. Probably feed men even in business suits, Heimrich had thought, as he tried the jacket on, with the uneasy feeling that he probably had widened out of it. He had not.)

There was room in the police car's trunk for all the bags. All the bags had tags on them—"S.S. Italia, 3/30, Cabin 82." There was ice on the drive outside the door. Merton Heimrich put an arm around his slim—no, damn it, "thin"—wife and helped her across the ice. He's ridiculous to worry so, Susan thought. He's not ridiculous. He is very dear.

They skidded only a little going down the steep driveway from the hilltop house. Eleven F was reasonably clear. "Warning: May be icy spots ahead." The Parkway had some puddles. They would be ice by midafternoon, if the Weather Bureau knew its business, which, from the coldness of the wind, it did. But they were going away from ice. In the back seat, Heimrich put an arm around Susan's shoulders and drew her against him. Susan turned to look up at him and smiled and said, "Yes. Isn't it?" although he had not said anything.

Traffic thickened on the Parkway and on the Henry Hudson. Below the George Washington Bridge it crept, and there was much horn-blaring as commuters churned toward offices. But they had counted on that. After they left the West Side Highway at Fifty-seventh Street, trucks loomed around them and air brakes hissed in front of them. But that, too, had been counted on. It was a little after ten when they pulled to a curb lined with men in green smocks with "Italian Line" across them in red.

The too many suitcases went on a truck. "No," Charley Forniss said. "No place to park it. Anyway, I've been on ships."

Charles Forniss had been a Marine Corps captain before he became a policeman. He'd been on ships. Forniss and Heimrich shook hands, although they were not hand-shaking types and, anyway, had shaken hands the day before. Forniss held both hands down to Susan, and she took them both, and he said, "Take care of yourself," and then, to Merton Heimrich, "Take care of her."

Heimrich said. "Sure. Mind the store, Charley," and he and Susan followed the man who pushed the luggage truck down a long, cold pier to a gangplank marked "First Class," and men in white jackets took cases off the trunk and disappeared while Heimrich tipped the longshoreman and went to a booth and gave tickets and their passports to a dark-haired young woman who, somewhat unexpectedly, said "*Grazie*." They went up the gangplank, and a tall man in a white jacket said, "Madame-sir-this-way-please." He put a hand, somewhat tenderly, on Heimrich's arm and guided. He guided into a line, but not a long line. The line led to a table with two men in uniform sitting behind it.

The man ahead of Heimrich in the line was almost as tall as Heimrich, but he was very thin. He had gray hair and the back of his neck was deeply tanned. The woman who walked beside him, as Susan walked beside Heimrich, wore a short mink coat.

The ship's officer at the end of the table had a plan in front of him—a plot of the ship's dining room. The tall thin man leaned down to him and said, "Grimes, Ronald. Table for two if you can manage it."

The tall man had a low voice and English intonation.

The officer next the one with the plan of the dining salon—"Salone da Pranzo Prima Classe" it had read on the deck plan which had come with the tickets—had typed sheets in front of him and ran a pencil down them. He said, "Cabins Sixteen and Eighteen, Sir Ronald?"

The tall gray-haired man merely nodded his head. The of-

15

ficer with the dining-salon plot in front of him looked over it. There were squares on the plot with four smaller squares around the sides. The officer drew pencil lines through two of the small squares at one of the large ones and said, "Table Twenty-two, Sir Ronald," and wrote "22" on a slip of paper and handed it to the tall thin man, who said, "Kew," and gave his place to Heimrich. The man with the typed passenger list looked at another, smaller list. He put a check mark on the larger list after the name "Grimes," and Heimrich gave his name. He did not give his first name, of which he disapproves. He said, "Mr. and Mrs. M. L. Heimrich. We asked our travel agent to arrange for a table for two."

Lists were consulted. The officer with the dining-room plan looked at it and found two more chairs to scratch from a table for four. He said, "Table Seventeen, Inspector."

It was not supposed to be "Inspector." It had been made clear to Miss Snell that "Mr. and Mrs. M. L. Heimrich" had booked passage on the S.S. *Italia*. "Inspector" invites questions, such as "What do you inspect, Inspector?" And the answer "Murder, chiefly," gets "Oh!" and, from the less reserved, inquiry for details.

Miss Snell had not listened. Of course, it did not too much matter.

They stopped and reserved deck chairs—on the enclosed promenade; starboard side by preference. They would be sailing south and east; the afternoon sun would fall to starboard. It would be good to sit in the sun again. Susan could do with the sun's warmth, even if sunlight came through glass.

Cabin 82?

"*Ponte superiore*, signor-signora. Upper deck, sir-madame. *Ascensore*, sir." And a gesture.

"How many floors up—I mean decks?" Susan said.

"One, signora."

They were at the foot of a wide staircase.

"We'd better—" Heimrich began and Susan said, "Nonsense. I'm fine," and he followed her up the staircase. There was a rail to hold onto, but Susan did not touch it.

They went down a wide passageway and, amidships, came to an open door marked "82." They went through a narrower corridor and passed shelves on which their suitcases were already stacked. They passed a closed door and were in a room larger than it had appeared to be from the plans they had studied in front of a fire in Van Brunt. There was a bed under two closed portholes; on the other side—against the inner wall (except that it would be a "bulkhead")—was a second bed. Between them there was a chest of drawers against one wall—no, *bulkhead*—and opposite it doors which opened on a closet spaces with a full-length mirror between them.

Susan looked around the room.

"You know," she said, "for the first time I believe it. Do you believe it, dear?"

"It feels real enough," Merton Heimrich said. "Are you all right, Susan?"

"I," Susan said. "am on holiday. Oh, I feel fine. We've never been on a ship together, have we? Nor, really—oh, on a holiday." She sat down on the bed under the portholes. She looked up at him.

"Actually," Susan said, "I feel wonderful. As if—oh, as if we ought to drink champagne."

"Only," Merton said, "neither of us much likes champagne."

"There is that," Susan said. "And it is also only a little after ten in the morning. But—don't you feel it too? As if—oh, as if everything were new?"

"I feel it too," Heimrich said, and went to sit on the bed beside his wife. He looked at her very carefully. Though they had got up too early and done last-minute packing and been driven into town on sometimes treacherous and at the end crowded roads, she didn't look so tired any more. When she smiled at him it was her smile.

They had not closed the cabin door. Sitting side by side on

17

the bed they could look through the passageway of Cabin 82 and into the corridor beyond it. People were moving in the corridor. Men in white jackets carried luggage through it; people huddled in overcoats walked through it and said, "*Here* we are," to one another. Bumping sounds came through a bulkhead from one of the cabins next to theirs. The *S.S. Italia* was filling up.

A dark-haired young woman, trim in white and green uniform, knocked at their open door and Susan said, "Yes?" and the young woman—the pretty young woman—came into the cabin. She said, "I am Angela, madame-sir. Your stewardess. Is there anything I can do for you?"

Her English was careful, precise. The intonation was British. There was nothing she could do for them.

"You have only to ring," Angela said. "Here." She pointed to buttons set into the wall above the dressing table. "I will come. Or Guido will come. He is the steward."

"Thank you," Susan said, and was almost as precise with words as Angela. "We'll ring when we need you."

"We are not going to Boston," Angela said. "There is a strike there. Those who were to have come aboard at Boston are coming here. We must wait for them, but they think it will not be long. Lunch will be served at one."

Susan said, "Thank you."

"You have but to ring," Angela said. "I will come or Guido will come. I can bring you ice?"

"No," Susan said. "Thank you, Angela."

The stewardess went down the passageway to the cabin door. She stopped at it and turned and said, "I shall close the door, yes? It is noisy. There is confusion."

There was not, particularly. There was order.

"If you will," Susan said, and Angela went out and closed the door behind her.

She seemed a nice girl. They agreed on that. They might as well start unpacking. They agreed on that. But for half an

18

hour they merely sat, secure, in that peace which comes when something long planned on and worried about and worked toward has come about. Susan put it into words. "We're really here," she said. "When the people from Boston come we'll sail away from winter."

She stubbed out her cigarette, making the action a period. They unpacked, hanging things in the wardrobes, putting things in drawers. Merton's dinner jacket had survived unwrinkled. Susan's dresses would shake out. They had finished, put cases back on shelves, when the ship began a gentle, just perceptible, vibration. "Engines on," Heimrich said, and Susan said, "Yes. It's coming alive, isn't it? We're really going on our holiday. Should we go somewhere—"

A loud hooting drowned her voice. It seemed to shake the ship. It stopped.

"—and watch?" Susan said.

They left the cabin and went along the corridor and climbed a flight of stairs. They went out on the promenade deck and, through glass, watched a pier move slowly past them. The ship hooted again as it backed into North River. It stopped and then, slowly, tugs nudging it and then dropping away, began to move forward. New York City began to drift past them.

"The cocktail lounge is on this deck," Heimrich said. "I remember that from the plan they sent us. And we're under way."

They found the cocktail lounge, which was very large and was open and was beginning to fill up. They found a table and ordered drinks, not of champagne, and when the drinks came they touched glasses, and Susan said, "Bon voyage to us both."

They had just finished the drinks when chimes sounded. Heimrich looked at a nearby bar steward, and the steward said, "Yes, signor. Luncheon is served. Shall I bring you and the signora another drink?"

They decided against that and, instructed, Heimrich wrote "82" on the bar slip.

19

They went down two decks in a small elevator and found the dining room, which stretched the width of the ship. They were guided to Table 17, which was set for two and from which they could see a long buffet table, with men in chef's hats behind it.

A waiter—no, steward—in a green jacket said, "Signor. Signora," on a note of triumph and put menus in front of them. The menus were enormous and in Italian and English, side by side. The menus were slightly overwhelming.

The steward said, "My name is Lorenzo, sir-madame. But Esposito, not de' Medici."

The Heimrichs disappointed Lorenzo, being content with omelets. ("No appetizer? No soup? But surely dessert, signora? The spumoni, perhaps? The wine steward, signor?")

Heimrich said, "Tonight, perhaps," to that, and Susan said, "Yes, spumoni, I think."

The four hearty women at the table next theirs, also served by Lorenzo, made up for the Heimrichs' abstinence. They started with shrimp cocktails and were resolute thereafter. Three of them had two desserts each.

After lunch, the Heimrichs went up to the promenade deck, by *ascensore*. On the starboard side the afternoon sun was shining through glass. A deck steward said, "Sir-madame," and found two deck chairs, side by side with the right names on them. The sun poured onto the chairs. The S.S. *Italia* seemed still in the quiet water, but looking down they could see the white froth of her bow wave. She lifted her prow gently against the ocean and dipped it gently.

There was an Italian lesson in the observation lounge on the boat deck. A bridge lesson was available in the card room, also on the boat deck—*ponte lance*. Shuffleboard was available on the belvedere deck. Tea would be served in the main cocktail lounge at four-thirty.

The Heimrichs sat in the sun, and the Atlantic drifted westward. At a little after four, Susan said, "I'm going down to the cabin and take a nap, if I can wake up enough to get there."

They went down to Cabin 82, and Susan chose as hers the bed on the outboard side, under the portholes. She undressed and got into it, and Heimrich thought, That's fine. She needs sleep. Sleep will be good for her. And then, I may as well lie down myself and be very quiet so as not to waken her.

When he himself awakened, it was after six, and her bed was empty. For a moment he was almost frightened, which was absurd. But for weeks he had been almost frightened. He went to the bathroom door and listened outside it and could hear the shower running.

He was surprised that he breathed in so deeply in relief. He got back into bed and lighted a cigarette and waited his turn.

ꙋ 2

It was a few minutes after seven when they went into the big cocktail lounge on the promenade deck. It was crowded. A great many other people were, apparently, on holiday. (Not on business, Susan thought. People on business flew in airplanes.) It was also noisy. And three men in red jackets roamed it, one carrying a guitar and one a violin and one only a tenor voice, of which he was making a great deal. (More, Susan thought, than it's worth.) Susan said, "Oh," in a diminished voice.

"There must be another," Heimrich said. "A quieter one. There must—hell, there're probably half a dozen. Wait."

They waited just inside the entrance. A captain in a dinner jacket beamed at them. He held up two fingers at them. He moved in front of a banquette space for two and beckoned.

On one side of the space he indicated, two men sat side by side, and one of them was smoking a cigar. On the other side two women sat together and they were, Heimrich thought, two of the four women who had had lunch at the table next theirs and had had two desserts apiece.

"I remember," Heimrich said. "On the boat deck, as I remember from the deck plan. All the way forward. Something called 'veranda belvedere.' The observation lounge, I think it is. It looked smaller on the plan."

He shook his head at the captain, who shrugged slightly and spread his hands and looked back with, it seemed to Merton Heimrich, understanding. Perhaps even with sympathy.

They found one of the neat small elevators. In it, Merton pressed the button lettered "Ponte Lance." The elevator closed its door and went up and stopped. They went through a passageway. They went past what appeared to be a small library. It was empty. They came into an uncrowded room with windows around it. Beyond the forward windows the bow of S.S. *Italia* gently rose and gently dipped.

There were sofas for two with tables in front of them and chairs grouped around tables, and there was a bar, and a lounge steward in a white jacket said, "Signor-signora," and waved a welcoming hand. There were no more than a dozen people in the room, which could have held fifty. Nobody was singing in the room, and the bow of the ship rose gently and subsided gently. There was a dance circle in the middle of the room, but nobody was dancing on it.

They sat on one of the little sofas so that they faced forward and could watch the slow rise, the slow dip, of the prow. It was a holiday ship again.

The steward stood in front of them. He said, "Sir? Madam?"

"Martinis," Merton Heimrich said. "Very dry. With a twist. Oh, and up."

The steward looked, Heimrich thought, slightly shocked. But he only said, "Certainly, sir," and went away. He was back almost before cigarettes were lighted. He put stemmed glasses down in front of them and a little dish with slivers of lemon peel. "I am Mario, sir," the steward said. "We chill the glasses." His speech was entirely American.

Susan twisted a lemon peel and put it in the ashtray. She

23

sipped from her glass. She put it down and nodded and said, "You're not as busy as they are downstairs." She considered. "I mean in the main cocktail lounge."

"First night out," Mario said. "Takes them a while to find us."

"Do the—er—musicians come here?" Heimrich asked.

Mario grinned. He had very white teeth in a tanned face. He shrugged his shoulders. "Sometimes," he said. He shrugged his shoulders, and his hands moved with the shrug. "Not tonight. Perhaps tomorrow night. People like to listen to them, sir."

There was nothing overt in his intonation. But Merton Heimrich, who listens to many voices and has an ear tuned to inflections, thought that Mario did not include himself among the people who liked to listen to the guitarist and the violinist and the singer.

He left them. He greeted a pretty, blue-eyed woman and the tall, thin man with gray hair who followed her into the *veranda belvedere*. Mario said, "Two, sir?" and the tall man shook his head and said, "Couple of friends probably be along."

They were taken to a table for four.

"They were just ahead of us when we came aboard," Susan said, leaning toward Merton, keeping her soft voice very low. "Sir somebody?"

"Sir Ronald Grimes," Merton said, in a voice which was so low a rumble even Susan could hardly make out the words. "And Lady Grimes, I suppose."

"It seems to me I've read something—" She paused. "We're staring. And probably they're thinking things about vulgar Americans. And thinking we call ourselves Am*u*ricans."

"They're across the room." Heimrich said. "They're ordering drinks. They're not thinking anything about us. And we're not staring. Read what?"

"Something about him," Susan said. "In—oh, in the *Times*.

24

U.N.? Was that it? Or Washington? Wait—member of the British delegation at the United Nations. Not the head of it. But answered the Russians once, I think. I don't remember what about."

"Capitalist imperialism," Heimrich said. "Almost certainly. As is well known."

"Would you say he's about fifty-five?" Susan wondered.

"Or a young sixty. Very fit, if so. Is your drink all right? And do you—"

He caught himself, but she smiled gaily at him and said, "I'm fine, dear. I'm really fine. So's the martini. And give me a cigarette."

"You're not supposed—"

But he looked at her and smiled back at her and shook a cigarette loose from the pack and flicked his lighter for her.

"Better," Susan said. "Much better. We're on holiday."

A very handsome—a very big and handsome—youngish man followed a slight young woman into the lounge. The man had a crisply barbered mustache. He had a rather long head. The girl was darkly pretty; her black hair fitted her small head like a cap. Mario met them and said, "Sir? Madam?" but the man raised a hand in greeting to Sir Ronald and, presumably, Lady Grimes, and he and the girl went across the room and joined the Grimeses at their table.

People drifted into the *veranda belvedere*. For the most part they came by twos. A substantial couple in, at a guess, their sixties—a smiling couple. They sat on a small sofa and ordered drinks and talked to each other with animation. In response to something the woman laughed and patted the man on his knee. Susan makes up stories about people in her mind. The smiling, substantial couple were celebrating their fortieth wedding anniversary. They had been talking to each other for forty years and still had much to say. That's fine, Susan thought. A much younger man and woman came in together and sat on a sofa together and did not seem to have

25

anything to say to each other. They're married too, Susan thought. They have run out of words for each other. That's too bad. Merton and I can be silent, drink and think our own thoughts. But, at another time, we have so many words for each other.

Four men came in together, and two of them were smoking cigars, and one of them looked around at the others in the lounge as if he were about to say, loudly, "Hello, everybody." They, Susan thought, are the spill-over from a convention. They are in the wholesale grocery business and live in California. But the four, after their drinks were served, began to talk rather loudly to one another, and they talked in French. So much for my intuition, Susan thought. She looked toward Merton, and he was turned toward her and smiling. He is getting over being worried about me, Susan Heimrich thought. It was dear of him to be so worried. I was not really worried; at the worst I was not really worried. Luck rides with us. The top of this table is not wood, but there is wood around the edges. She tapped the wood gently with her finger tips.

"Yes," Merton Heimrich said and knocked on wood.

Mario stood in front of them and looked down at empty glasses and said, "Sir? Madam?"

"Yes," Heimrich said. "They're very good, Mario."

"The bartender used to be at the Italian Pavilion," Mario said. "I was a waiter at the Saint Regis for quite a while. There I was Henri."

He went away.

There were two men behind the bar by then, but only Mario serving in front of it. The room still was not crowded, but there were a good many people in it.

"He can be more than two places at once," Susan said. "He can be four places at once. Mario, I mean."

A woman came in alone. She was slender and elegant in dinner pajamas, and a silver-white streak ran artfully through her black hair. She is older than she wants to be, Susan thought.

26

If she smiled her face would break into pieces—would shatter. She is waiting for the rest of the party, but there isn't any rest of the party. The rest of the party went somewhere else long ago. Two men and two women came in, and the woman in pajamas looked at them as if they were the friends she was expecting, but they went to another table for four. I can't make up any stories at all about them, Susan thought, and Merton said, "Thanks, Mario," for new drinks.

They were halfway through their second round when chimes sounded. "The dinner bell," Heimrich said, and looked at his watch. "Yes. Just eight."

The four men who had been speaking French, not Californian, finished off their drinks. The one who had seemed about to issue a general greeting stood up and crushed his cigar down into an ashtray. He said, *"Garçon,"* and spoke rather loudly, because Mario was at the other side of the room, and was putting drinks down on a table. The standing man pointed and said, "You! Waiter!"

Mario crossed the room, very white teeth showing through a somewhat set smile. The four men put cabin numbers on separate checks and got up and walked out. The ship was moving a little now. One of the men clutched at the back of a chair in which a pretty young woman was sitting. He said, *"Pardon,"* more loudly than was really necessary.

"Hungry types," Merton Heimrich said. "In resort hotels they wait outside dining-room doors. Whatever hour dinner is, they're there at a quarter of."

"They were talking French," Susan said.

"All right," Merton Heimrich said. "French resort hotels. French hungry types."

Nobody else in the lounge had responded to the chimes. But then the woman with the white streak through her black hair looked at the watch on her wrist and then shook her wrist with resentment and stood up. Mario was there at once; she wrote on a check; she went out of the room.

27

"Stood up?" Heimrich asked his wife. Susan shook her head.

"What we're supposed to think," Susan said. "Only—only I'm afraid she was stood up years ago, aren't you? When—oh, when the party went away and left her." She sipped from her glass. "Our party won't go away, will it, Merton?"

"Not ever," Merton said. "When you knocked on wood a few minutes ago?"

"Yes," Susan said. "That was why. And because those two —" she moved her head slightly toward the two she meant— "haven't anything to say to each other. Or am I not being clear, darling?"

"Very clear," he told her.

Sir Ronald Grimes stood up at his table. He pulled his wife's chair away from it, and they went across the room and through a doorway. The big younger man who had joined them stood up as Lady Grimes stood. But then he sat down again and held up two fingers toward Mario and circled them over empty glasses. He leaned toward the girl with the polished cap of hair and began to talk to her, and she laughed.

A thin, not tall, man got up from a table at which he had sat alone, and put a number on his bar check and went out of the room. Susan had not made up any story about him. He had been there, sitting alone, drinking a tall drink. But she had not seen him or wondered about him. Some people, she thought, are invisible until they move.

They finished their drinks and went down to the dining room. They went down by the broad staircase because, at each of the elevators, little groups of people were waiting. The ship was moving now, but slowly, thoughtfully. They held to bannisters going down the stairs. In the dining room the deck moved gently under their feet. Lorenzo saw them coming; he pulled out chairs for them. He said, "Signor. Signora," and gave them menus. He said, "This evening the wine steward, sir?"

They looked at each other. It was Susan, who, after a moment, nodded her head. She said, "Holiday."

The menu, which had been large for lunch, had grown for dinner. "There is," Susan said, "nothing like doing nothing all day to build up the appetite."

The stalwart women at the next table were finishing soup. The one who finished first looked intently at Lorenzo and then, abruptly, beckoned. He went to them. "Roast beef," the woman said. "If it's well done. And spaghetti, I think. With the meat sauce."

Lorenzo said, "Signora."

The other women ordered, making the best of abundance. The waiter smiled. He said, "Signora. Signora." He made a list and beckoned another steward, who wore a white jacket with green lapels. A lesser steward, in the hierarchy of stewards. The lesser steward said, "Sir," and went down the long room. Lorenzo, of the entirely green jacket, returned to the Heimrichs. He said, "Signor? Signora?"

They ordered, more ambitiously than they had at lunch. "The sea air, no doubt," Merton Heimrich said. Lorenzo smiled down at them, encouraging. Asked about something which was identical in Italian and in English he said, "Veal with peppers, signor. Excellent." When they had ordered, he said "Signor, signora" again, with gratification. He said, "I will send the wine steward." He went away. The steward with green lapels returned. He filled their water glasses.

A steward in a yellow jacket came to their table. He did not have the sommelier's dangling keys. But he had a plaque on the left-hand pocket of his jacket, and the disk was embossed with wine bottles, their necks crossed. He said, "The wine list, signor," and gave a long, stiff sheet to Merton Heimrich.

There were a great many wines listed on it—a confusingly great many wines.

The wine steward was gentle. He said. "The lady and gentleman have ordered?"

They had ordered. Heimrich told him what.

"A white I would recommend," the steward said. "By all means a white, signor."

He is used to guiding the innocent, Susan thought. The bewildered.

"If I may suggest," the steward said. "The Soave Bolla is an excellent wine. A very good year, if I may say so, signor."

"If it isn't sweet," Susan said.

The steward shrugged, apparently in horror. He spread his hands. "Soft," he said. "But dry. An admirable wine. The late Somerset Maugham always ordered it."

Something, Merton Heimrich thought, seemed to been jumped. He said, "Here? On this ship?"

"I do not know, signor. At the Gritti Palace. In Venezia." He raised his hands again and, of each, coupled index finger and thumb. "He wrote about it in their brochure. About the Soave Bolla. About the hotel, also."

"You met him there?" Susan asked. "Waited on him?"

The wine steward shook his head, sadly. "He was before my time at the Gritti," he said. "It is a magnificent hotel. On the Canal. The Soave Bolla, signor?"

"A half bottle?"

"I regret, signor. We have no half bottles. But if you do not finish the bottle, it will be reserved for you, signor. It will be on your table tomorrow."

The food was delicious. The Soave Bolla all that had been promised. "Ah," Heimrich said. "The bouquet, n'est ce pas?" They laughed softly across the table. Crêpes suzette were not on the menu, but a man in dinner jacket was making them within sight. Lorenzo, consulted, said, "But certainly, madame."

The crêpes were good. The espresso was sharp and bitter, and there were strips of lemon rind to twist and drop into it.

For a time they sat in their deck chairs, but there was no sun now, and the sea which stretched around the ship was a dark sea. Music came from somewhere, and they went toward the music. They came to double doors with "Salone delle Feste" on a softly illuminated sign above them. An orchestra was playing, a little loudly, and a few couples were dancing on a circular floor in the middle of a large room. There were many chairs around many tables. Stewards moved, carrying trays. A man in a dinner jacket said, "Signor? Signora?"

Heimrich looked down at his wife. She looked fine. But still—

"It's been a long day," Susan said. "A holiday, but a long day. Tomorrow?"

They went down to Cabin 82. The beds had been turned down. Water poured from carafes set in restraining hoops was cold.

"A beautiful holiday," Susan said, in a sleepy voice as Merton leaned down to kiss her good night. "A most won—"

But sleep overtook the word.

Heimrich wakened first. He went across the cabin and leaned over Susan's bed so he could look through one of the portholes. The sun glinted on quiet water. Now the ship seemed, as it had at first, almost stationary in the water. But by craning his neck a little, Merton Heimrich could see the froth of her bow wave.

"Is it a nice day, darling?" Susan said up to him.

"A fine day," Heimrich said. "I tried to be quiet."

"You were very quiet," Susan told him. "They'll bring us breakfast here, won't they?"

Heimrich pressed a button marked "Steward." On second thought, he also pressed one marked "Stewardess." He saw paper under the cabin door and collected the passenger list and a square white envelope addressed, "Inspector and Mrs. M. L. Heimrich."

Comandante Antonio di Scarlotti and the Officers of S.S. *Italia* requested the pleasure of the company of Inspector and Mrs. M. L. Heimrich for cocktails in the main lounge at seven P.M.

Their names were written in where a suitable blank oc-

31

curred. The rest of the invitation was, Merton discovered by running a finger over it, engraved.

On the passenger list, their names were correctly spelled. But it was, as Heimrich had been uneasily certain it would be, "Inspector and Mrs." Not, as he had asked Miss Snell, "Mr. and Mrs." So.

It was Sir Ronald Grimes, Bart., and Lady Grimes. There were no other names either recognized. "I knew an Elsie Singleton once," Susan said. "But I'm almost sure she's dead." "I arrested a George Larsen once," Heimrich said. "But he's still in prison, far as I know."

It was the steward who knocked at the door and, being invited, came into the cabin. He said, "I am Guido, signor-signora. It is a fine morning. I may bring you breakfast, sì?"

They ordered. When breakfast came, in a surprisingly short time, it was Angela who came first into the room, balancing a tray on upheld fingers. Guido came after her. The coffee was hot and strong, Heimrich's bacon crisp and his scrambled eggs soft. Croissants came with Susan's coffee. They were warm and buttery and crunched between the teeth.

"This is a lovely ship," Susan said. "We've landed on our feet, haven't we?"

Merton Heimrich agreed they had landed on their feet. He added that it was a habit they must cultivate.

ꙮ 3

It was a day for lolling. Sunshine had not reached their deck chairs when they went to them, but it shone on the ocean. The sliding glass panel forward of where they sat was a little open, and the air which came through it was balmy. "It's so soon for it to be spring," Susan said, and was told it had been spring for almost two weeks. She said, "Where we live it's sometimes spring by the middle of May," a statement which could not be argued with. At eleven, stewards brought consommé and small, neat sandwiches. In the *veranda belvedere* before lunch, Mario knew what they wanted before they ordered it. On their table in the dining room, the newly chilled remainder of a bottle of Soave Bolla waited them. At the table next theirs all four of the stalwart women had two desserts.

The sun was warm on the chairs in the afternoon. They avoided Italian lessons and bridge lessons and shuffleboard and deck tennis. "I ought to write letters to people," Susan said, and did not move. She was told, sleepily, that letters would go nowhere until they reached Lisbon. Susan agreed that there was that. She said, "We ought to walk around the deck or

33

something. There's a gymnasium or something, isn't there? I'll get fat, won't I?"

"No," Merton told her. "You'll never get fat. And just now you could do—"

"I'm fine," Susan said. "I think I'll go to the cabin and take a nap." They both went to the cabin and took naps. Some time during the naps bells rang, and there were footsteps in the corridor outside Cabin 82, but they did not really waken. Merton was showering when he remembered that Boat Drill had been scheduled for four, and that all passengers were urged—resolutely urged—to attend, wearing life preservers. They were to follow arrows to their rallying points. So that was what the bells had been about.

At seven, Susan said, "You look fine. We ought to dress for dinner every night."

"Well," Merton said, "we do light candles most nights."

"Not most," she said. "Most nights you are chasing murderers. Stand still and I'll straighten your tie. It lists a little. To starboard, I think it is."

She reached up and straightened his black bow tie. She said, "Of course it will stay. We're on holiday."

"We'll be the first to arrive," Merton said, as they went up in an elevator because Susan's dress was long and not designed for the climbing of stairs. "It's only ten after."

They were not the first to arrive. They were not even, at a guess, the hundredth. Inside the lounge a row of officers stood, in white uniforms with shoulder boards. The two officers at the head of the line had four stripes across their shoulder boards. From there on the number of stripes diminished. The last in the line had only a single stripe, and it was narrower.

Beyond the officers, the lounge seethed with people. Beyond the people was a long bar. There was not, it was at once apparent, going to be any place to sit down.

The maître d' was just inside the entrance. He said, "Signor Inspector. Signora," and stepped aside, and a man with a camera flashed at them. "If you will, please," the maître d'

34

said. "This way, please." They moved a few steps to the reception line of officers. "Signora—" the maître d' said and stopped. Everything cannot be perfect, even on a holiday. "Heimrich," Susan said. "Comandante di Scarlotti," the maître d' said. "Inspector Heimling, Comandante."

"Pleasure, signora," Comandante di Scarlotti said. "Pleasure, Inspector."

He bowed over Susan's hand. His hand was firm in Merton's. He was tall and dark-haired and stood erect. And he had eyes as blue as Heimrich's own. Somewhat unexpectedly, he said, "Welcome aboard, signora, signor." And his hand propelled them on. "Comandante Ferrancci,"the maître d' said. "Signora Heimberg. Inspector Heimberg."

Perfection is unlikely even on a lovely ship.

Comandante Ferrancci was even taller than Comandante di Scarlotti. His eyes were level with Heimrich's own. He was younger than the other comandante. He was a very handsome man, and he had a crisp blond mustache and blond hair, cut short but with a ripple in it. He bowed over Susan's hand; he grasped Heimrich's firmly. He said, "But it's Heimrich, isn't it, Inspector? Not—what did Lucien call you?"

"Heimrich," Heimrich said. "It doesn't matter, Captain."

Ferrancci said, "Welcome aboard, Inspector."

They came to the end of the line of officers—came, at any rate, near the end before the maître d' said, "Excuse me, signora-signor," and went back to welcome more guests to a party which already had more than enough guests.

Susan and Merton Heimrich were jostled into the crowd, through which waiters with trays sorted their way. A round, red-faced man with a glass swaying in his hand confronted Heimrich. He said, "If it isn't old Ned Farmer. Good old Ned way off here on—"

"No," Heimrich said. "I'm not good old Ned Farmer."

He was looked at blankly.

"Got to be," the round man said. "Pretending to be good old Ned Farmer. Not a damn bit like him and you know it."

35

"Heimling, his name is," Susan said. "Come on, Mr. Heimling. Good-by, Mr. Farmer."

Words and sentences come out of a crowd—come out lonely and with no context. "On the way back from Nassau—" came out of the crowd, on a male voice. They did not wait to hear about the way back from Nassau. "It was our fifth," rode out of the crowd on a woman's carrying voice. "I gave him a one-way ticket to Europe as an anniversary present."

Susan looked up at Merton Heimrich, and he looked down at her. Both raised their eyebrows; both shook their heads.

The nearest exit now was across the room and through a multitude. They made it.

"I don't think there's anybody we know here," Susan said. "Let's go up and see Mario. And sit down and have a quiet drink."

The *veranda belvedere* was not empty. There were, it was evident, others who preferred to drink sitting down. Mario was everywhere, as he had been before. But he was free to greet the Heimrichs, to say, "Madam-sir," being in an American mood, and to lead them to a small sofa behind a table and facing the dance floor, on which nobody was dancing. He said, "I remember, sir. As before, sir?"

"As before," Heimrich said, and Mario said, "O.K., Inspector," and went away.

And the tall, very thin man with gray hair on the sofa next theirs, with the pretty blond woman who wore evening pajamas with blue in them which matched her eyes, turned to Heimrich and said, "Inspector Heimrich? Thought it might be, y'know."

"Yes, Sir Ronald," Heimrich said.

"Heard of you," Ronald Grimes said. "Try to sort people out. You do too, apparently. This is my wife, Inspector."

Heimrich said, "Lady Grimes." He said, "Mrs. Heimrich."

"Bit of a brawl down below," Sir Ronald said. "Always is, come to that. Ellen and I give them a miss. Won't be another this voyage, y'know. There's always that."

36

There had not been time for it, but Mario arrived with drinks.

"Something of a miracle, our Mario," Sir Ronald said. "Always has been. Cheers. Or do you Americans say, 'Down the hatch'?"

"None I've ever known," Susan said. "Do the English say, 'What-what'?"

Ellen Grimes laughed. She had light, clear laughter. She said, "Only in Wodehouse. I think. Oh, perhaps a generation ago. A restful voyage so far, Mrs. Heimrich? *Italia's* a pleasant ship, we think."

"Very restful," Susan said, and thought it chitchat. But, on the whole, the Grimeses' chitchat. "You've been on this ship before, I gather?"

"From time to time," Sir Ronald said. "When there was time to spare." He spoke lightly, and smiled at them. But then he said, "Now there's all the time in the world, y'know" His voice was different on the last words. The lightness had gone out of it. "Flew back and forth a bit in the old days."

"When you were in Washington," Susan said. "Or at the U.N." She paused for a moment. Then she said, "You see, we've heard of you too, Sir Ronald."

"Can't imagine how," Ronald Grimes said. "No top jobs. Nothing like that. On my way to pasture now. Mandatory in the service. End up growing roses, shouldn't wonder. Or, come to that, cabbages." His voice was light again. Then he raised it. He said, "Oh, Bert. Colleague of yours here."

A slight, middle-aged man was following Mario across the dance floor, toward a small table with a single chair. He stopped and turned. He was the man they had seen leave a similar small table the evening before, just after the Grimeses had left the younger couple at the table they had shared. "Bert" was the man who was invisible until he moved.

He stopped his progress toward the table and turned to them and said, "Evening."

"Detective Inspector Albert Hunt, Heimrich," Grimes

37

said. "Inspector Heimrich, Hunt. New York State Police. That right, Heimrich?"

"That's right," Heimrich said and reached across the table to take Hunt's reticently extended hand. "Evening, Inspector."

"After malefactors, Bert?" Grimes said. "Or just—"

He left it hang.

"Man in New York we wanted a word with," Hunt said. "Nothing important, Sir Ronald."

"Join us?" Grimes said.

Hunt shook his head. "Just time for a quick one, sir," he said. "Working on a report. Better get on with it. Pleasure to meet you, Inspector." He half bowed to Susan. He went on to the table by which Mario waited.

"Good chap, from all I hear," Grimes said. "Ran into him in London last time I was there. Little matter came up. Trivial, really. Hunt straightened it out in no time."

The dinner chimes sounded. Ronald Grimes turned to his wife. He said, "What say, m'dear?"

Lady Grimes's glass was still half full. She emptied it and said, "Of course, Ronald." Her voice was as light and clear as her laughter had been. Grimes stood up and pushed back the little sofa, and the two of them stood for a moment looking down at the Heimrichs.

"Been a pleasure, y'know," Grimes said. "See you about, probably."

Heimrich stood up. He made agreeing sounds. Sir Ronald Grimes, Bart., followed Lady Grimes out of the *veranda belvedere*. Heimrich sat down again to his barely touched martini.

"Supposed to be stand-offish," Susan said. "Reserved and all that sort of thing. She's very pretty, isn't she?"

"Very," Heimrich said.

"And," Susan said, "about twenty years younger than he is, wouldn't you say?"

"That would be putting her at forty, since he's probably sixty. She's more like thirty-five, I'd say."

"And he's retired, I gather. Going home to grow roses. Or perhaps cabbages. On the ancestral acres."

"If any."

"He's a baronet," Susan said. "Baronets always have an cestral acres. They just missed their friends."

Heimrich raised his eyebrows.

"The couple they were with last night," Susan said. "A big man with a mustache. A girl with black hair. He looked like—"

"I remember," Heimrich said. "Missed them?"

"They just came in," Susan said. "Through the other en trance. I mean, the one the Grimeses didn't go out through. If one can go out through an entrance."

"Quite possible, I'd think," Heimrich said, and looked the way Susan was looking. The girl's hair still fitted like a black cap. Mario met them. He took them to a small sofa on the other side of the dance floor.

"Lady Grimes hadn't finished her drink," Susan said. "Hadn't nearly finished. He—did he hurry them off, Merton?"

"Possibly," Merton Heimrich said. "Probably he was just hungry."

Mario paused in front of them.

"Please," Heimrich said and circled a finger over empty glasses.

Mario said, "Sir-madam," and took the empty glasses away.

"Isn't he small to be a policeman?" Susan said.

"Hunt? A little, perhaps. I don't know the English standards. You're very observant tonight, Susan."

"Oh," she said, "new people. I make up stories about new people. You know that. As you—as you find out old stories about them. The Grimeses go away rather suddenly. To avoid the people they were with last night and—"

"And Hunt is small to be a policeman," Heimrich said. "And we're on holiday, my darling."

39

She looked at him, smiling. She said, "I think you ought to wear a dinner jacket all the time."

At dinner that night they ordered another bottle of Soave Bolla. This night they drank more of it. After dinner they did not go to deck chairs or to the *salone delle feste.* They went to Cabin 82. This night they were not so sleepy . . .

The ship's newspaper was under the cabin door the next morning. On the front page was a picture of last night's cocktail party in the main lounge. It was a picture of a lot of people dressed for the evening. Under the door was also a square white envelope, addressed to Inspector and Mrs. M. L. Heimrich.

"Not again," Susan said, when Merton gave it to her to open. "I thought it was one of a—oh."

She handed the stiff white paper enclosure to Merton. It was "again," but different. This time Comandante Antonio di Scarlotti requested the pleasure of their company for cocktails in his "sitting room." The time was seven.

It was sunny again that third day out; the ship had, it appeared, altered course slightly. By ten in the morning sunlight slanted across their deck chairs. The glass panel near them had been slid a little farther open. The air which came in was a little warmer. They stretched in the sun and talked and sat silent. Susan hoped Michael was all right. Merton was sure Michael was all right. And that Colonel and Mite were all right. "Colonel will be morose. He will be very sad."

But most of the time Colonel is very sad. He is a mournful dog.

Consommé and small sandwiches came at eleven. This time they both ate sandwiches. "We're eating a lot more than we do at home," Susan said. "Drinking more, if it comes to that. Wine, too." Merton said, "Holiday," in a sleepy voice but then turned in his chair so that he could look at his wife.

It was being good for her. he thought. Already it was being

good for her. There was color in her face which had not been there for weeks. The line of tiredness was disappearing from around her eyes.

"Yes," Susan said, "it's being good for me, dear. It's being very good for me. I'm beginning to feel like a different person."

"The one you were was fine."

"That one again, then," Susan said. "Do you want to go up—I mean above—to the boat deck and walk in the air?"

The answer to that was simple. "No," Heimrich said. "Tomorrow, perhaps. Day after tomorrow. It will be warmer day after tomorrow."

Susan supposed so. But after five minutes, during which they both looked lazily at the Atlantic Ocean—which did not seem itself as lazy this day as it had the day before—Susan swung around on her chair and swung to her feet. She moves better than she's been moving, Heimrich thought. The spring is back in her. Dr. Forbes knew what—

"I," Susan said, "am going above and walk around the deck. Breathe the ocean air. Walk twice around the ship. Have— what do they call it?—a constitutional. Are you coming?"

The answer was simple again. It was the same answer. He added to it, "On Italian ships you don't take constitutionals. That's on British ships. On British ships, also, you take cold showers."

He was sitting inboard. He got up and moved his chair out of her way and, when she had passed, sat down again.

"Lazy," Susan Heimrich said.

"It was a long hard winter," Merton told her. "The ship's moving more today. Don't fall off."

"There's a railing," she said. "I'll hold onto the railing."

He watched her walk away along the deck to a door. The ship was moving more; it was rolling a little. She moved surely, balancing with the ship. She went in through the door, and Heimrich turned in his chair and watched the Atlantic.

41

He sat too low to see the froth of the bow wave, but the ship vibrated comfortingly. Everything was fine. Most of all, Susan was fine.

She was gone almost half an hour. and it was only during the last five minutes or so that he began to worry. But she came back through the door and down the ship to him, and her crisp brown hair had been blown, and there was color in her face and a new brightness in her eyes.

"Wonderful," she said, and pulled a blanket around her as she sat in the deck chair. "Sea air is all it's supposed to be. Only a little cooler than I'd thought. And the rail is quite high, so nobody could possibly fall off. But you didn't really think I'd fall off, did you?"

"No. Oh, I consider all possibilities. Part of the trade. But, on the whole, no."

He looked at his watch.

"Yes," Susan said. "It's open. I walked past and looked in the windows. Up there the ship seems to go up and down more than it does here."

"Habit they have. We're pretty much amidships. Forward, we'll notice the motion more. Shall we go see Mario?"

It was only noon. Susan looked at her watch and mentioned that it was only noon.

"Over the yardarm," Heimrich said. "Whatever a yardarm may be. But there's no hurry. There's no hurry about anything."

"Not about anything," Susan said. "Remember the woman whose party didn't come?"

Heimrich shook his head.

"Last night," Susan said. "Tall. Slim. In dinner pajamas from a good place. Bergdorf's, at a guess. Blue, mostly, with yellow accents. Flared out the ankles. All dressed up for a party, really. But no party. Of course you remember."

"No."

"At a table by herself," Susan said. "A little too much

make-up, I thought. Kept looking as if she were expecting somebody. Black hair with a white streak through it. Art, not nature. You *must* remember, dear. And there's no use saying you don't look at people, because you do look at people."

"All right," Heimrich said. "I remember somebody like that. In the Belvedere. Went out early. Why, Susan?"

"I bumped into her," Susan said. "Literally. Rather, she bumped into me. Going around a bend, and the ship swayed. The way it's doing now."

S.S. *Italia* was rolling a little. Not inconveniently, but a little.

"And?"

"Nothing, really. A very small bumping together. She was very sorry. So very, *very* sorry. And it was all her fault. Which was true enough, but not important. Only, she made a great deal of it. And she told me her name and wanted to know what mine was as if—oh, almost as if our cars had bumped into each other and she was showing her driver's license and wanted to see mine. Information-for-the-insurance-company sort of thing. But she'd hardly bumped into me at all, and I kept telling her that."

Heimich said that people were that way sometimes.

"I thought last night that she was lonely," Susan said. "That the party had gone away and left her. I think she's very lonely, Merton. Wants somebody to talk to. Do you suppose?"

"No," Heimrich said. "No lame dogs over stiles."

"She's a Mrs. Powers," Susan said. "Mrs. Raymond Powers. Her husband died about a year ago. Ought the name to mean something special?"

"Not to me it doesn't."

"She made it sound as if it should," Susan said. "As if I were supposed to say, 'Not *the* Raymond Powers.' I think I disappointed her."

"She seems to have been outgoing," Heimrich said. "She didn't say, 'Not *the* Mrs. Heimrich,' I hope."

43

Susan shook her head, laughing a little.

"We walked around part of the ship together," she said. "She's from Chicago, originally. Recently, until her husband's death, they'd been living in Washington. Was he a senator or something, do you suppose? Somebody we really ought to know about."

"I doubt it," Heimrich said. "From what you say of her, she'd have made a point of it if he'd been a senator."

He looked at his watch again.

"All right," Susan said. "We don't want to keep Mario waiting."

They climbed to the boat deck and the open promenade. There the breeze was brisk and cool, but it felt like a breeze of spring. The ship seemed to be moving faster, and her prow rose and sank more rapidly than it had the day before.

"We can walk right around in front of the observation lounge," Susan said. "The Belvedere. It's where Mrs. Powers and I bumped into each other. We can go in on the other side."

Heimrich had stopped at the nearest door and reached out to pull it open. But Susan went on, and he followed her; caught up with her. The deck rail was high enough; substantial enough. But he had not really worried. Forward of the lounge, the wind was stronger. As they rounded the lounge's curving windows, the wind blew them back along the port side. It ruffled Susan's hair and, suddenly, about nothing, Susan was laughing. He was laughing with her as he tugged the door open, and they went into the windless quiet of the lounge's lobby. Susan smoothed her blown hair down with thin hands. But her hands were not as thin as they had been weeks before.

They went along a short corridor. On one side of if the door to the ship's library stood open. There were bookshelves with books on them, and nobody was in the room. Opposite that door there was another, opening to an even smaller compartment. A sign above it said, "Sala Scrittura. Writing Room." There was a man in it with a briefcase open in front of him on a desk. He was consulting documents from the briefcase and making notes. He was also smoking a cigar. Like, Merton Heimrich thought, a man on the 8:04 from Cold Harbor who has taken his work home with him.

They went on into the observation lounge, and there were very few in the lounge—a couple at the starboard side, intent on each other and on their drinks; the four men with cigars, still talking French rather loudly; drinking pink liquid from small glasses. Mario said, "Signor Inspector! Signora!" with enthusiasm, with what appeared to be surprised delight. He took them to the sofa for two they had occupied the noon before. He said, "As before, madam, sir?"

"I—" Susan said, but by then Mario had gone to the bar.

"I had," Susan said, "been thinking of a very dry sherry."

Heimrich turned and looked toward the bar and started to raise a summoning hand, but Susan said, "Not really too seriously, dear. And we don't want to hurt Mario's feelings."

Behind them there was the faint clatter of ice against glass.

"Anyway," Susan said, "it's too late now, isn't it?" She sounded pleased, as one does when succumbing to temptation.

Mario brought their drinks, and they clicked glasses. When they had sipped from them, Susan looked again around the room. She said, "He's the easiest man to miss, isn't he? The lowest visibility possible."

Heimrich looked in the direction she was looking in.

Detective Inspector Albert Hunt was sitting by himself at a small table. He had a tall glass in front of him and was looking across the dance floor at the Heimrichs. Merton Heimrich flicked a hand toward a colleague and returned it to his glass.

Hunt flicked a hand in answer and smiled. It was not an

45

emphatic smile. He looked at his glass as if he were consulting it and took a sip from it and put it down again. Then he pushed his chair back a little, as if he were about to stand up. Susan looked at her husband and raised her eyebrows and said, her voice just audible, "Coming over to say hello?"

It was possible. It was difficult to tell. But then Hunt looked across the lounge, toward the doorway the Heimrichs had come through, and sat down again and raised his glass, holding it in front of his face and drinking from it.

Mrs. Raymond Powers came into the room, alone. She was wearing a suit, and the streak of white was immaculate in her black hair. As she followed Mario across the room, she saw the Heimrichs and nodded her head and smiled. The smile was a formality, and a faint one. She was led to a table for four and sat alone at it; sat where she could look around the room. She is still waiting for the party which doesn't come, Susan thought. Waiting for—

She suddenly put her hand on Merton's. He smiled at her and raised inquiring eyebrows.

"Because you're here," she said. "It would be bad if you weren't. It would be very lonely, dear. I'd—I'd wait for a party which didn't come."

The tall, handsome, youngish man with the crisp mustache whom they had first seen with the Grimeses came into the room. The girl with the smooth cap of black hair was not with him. Mario leaned over his table and said, "Sì, signor," and went away.

"Where did he go?" Susan said, and Heimrich said, "Did who—?" and looked across the dance floor. Hunt had disappeared from the table, and Heimrich said, "Oh. To work on that report of his, probably."

"I thought," Susan said, "he was going to come over and say something to us. To you, really. He was looking at you."

"If so," Merton Heimrich said, "he changed his mind."

"When Mrs. Powers came in," Susan said. "And the friend of the Grimeses came right after her."

46

"You're making up stories," he told her.

"My weakened condition," Susan said, and finished her drink. They were good martinis, but rather small ones. Because they were such small drinks, they had another round and went down, by elevator, to the foyer deck and the dining room and their steward, Lorenzo, who beamed at them and pulled out chairs for them and gave them menus which were as varied and large as usual.

They were reading menus when the maître d' stopped at their table. He was in a dinner jacket, and he wore a starched shirt, which set him apart from the mere captains, who wore soft shirts with their dinner jackets. He said, "Inspector? Signora?" They looked up at him and waited.

"You are having cocktails with the comandante this evening," the maître d' said. "It is not so?"

"He was good enough to ask us," Susan said, using phrasing suitable to a starched dress shirt.

The maître d' said, "Ah." Then he said, "In the main lounge? At seven? I will meet you there? You and the others, sì? I will escort you to the comandante's quarters?"

"Yes," Heimrich said to all the questions. He decided that saying it once would be adequate.

♨ 4

To Susan it had the feel of a special party. "A V.I.P. party," she said. She was told that if it were a V.I.P. party they wouldn't be going, would not have been invited. "After all," Heimrich told her, putting on a white shirt, considering the intricacies of tying a black bow tie, "I'm a cop. Not even a city cop." He was told not to be ridiculous; he was told that he was an inspector of police, which was V.I.P. enough for anyone. He was told Susan thought that, under the circumstances, she would wear her "new" dress.

The "new" dress was rather a special dress. Susan's designs are for decorator's fabrics—for curtains, for slip covers. Standing before her easel in early fall, Susan had had in mind something very special in slip-cover material—something gay and swirling with color. But as poster paint went on drawing board, slip-cover fabric had not come of it. The colors swirled; the colors danced. But nobody was going to use it to slip-cover a sofa. What it comes to, Susan thought, is that I've designed a dress fabric—a fabric for someone very young and gay who can carry it off. I wish—

48

She had had it printed, but not on "gray goods" for furniture fabric. It had come out beautifully. She had stroked the soft material and held it up against her and had thought, If only I were gay enough and young enough. She had taken the material to a dressmaker, and the dress fitted Susan Heimrich beautifully. She had tried it on for Merton and had said, "Do you think it's too—oh, too something?"

"I," Heimrich had said, "think it's a knockout." He had looked at her, standing in front of the fire in the living room in Van Brunt. "Also," he had said, "I think you're lovely."

It was a dinner dress and meant for summer, and there had, that brutal winter, been no occasion for a summery dinner dress. But she had brought it along on their holiday, and now, while Heimrich knotted his black tie and pulled it loose and knotted it again—and swore at it, not particularly under his breath—Susan got the dress out and held it up and looked at it. It had shaken out beautifully. She thought, Of course it is too something. I'm not up to my dress. And she put the dress on.

"This damned thing—" Heimrich said, turning from the mirror, "is—whew!" He looked at her carefully. "Yes," he said. "Indeed yes. You'll make it very V.I.P. Did I ever tell you you're—"

"Yes," she said. "You do exaggerate, dear. Stand still and let me tie your tie."

They went above, to the promenade deck and into the main lounge, and it was precisely seven o'clock. At the forward end of the lounge the maître d', still in a stiff white shirt but now with a white dinner jacket over it, was sitting very upright on a very upright chair. He was facing toward a sofa and toward Mrs. Raymond Powers, who was in a black sheath dinner dress which, Susan decided, did a lot for her. It appeared, from a distance, that the maître d' had said something amusing, because Mrs. Powers was smiling widely at him.

The maître d' looked away from Mrs. Powers and her ap-

49

preciating smile. He looked down the lounge and from side to side of it. He saw the Heimrichs coming and was on his feet. They were still some distance from him when he said, "Inspector. Signora." Then, Susan thought inadvertently, he looked at the watch on his wrist. The captain must be a martinet, Susan thought. If we are late he'll probably have the maître d' reduced to bus boy.

"Mrs. Heimberg," he told Mrs. Raymond Powers, with a flourish in his voice. "Inspector Heimberg. Mrs. Powers. Mrs. Raymond Powers."

Mrs. Powers smiled, all grace. She held out a hand to Susan. "Mrs. Heimrich and I have met," she said. She was careful with the name. "Good evening, Inspector."

The Heimrichs sat, Susan beside Mrs. Powers. The maître d' remained standing, looking anxiously down the room. He looked at his watch again. Then he said, "Ah!" with relief in his tone and then, to a substantial woman in a gray dress, he said, "Miss Farwell!"

She was one of the women at the table next the Heimrichs'. She was one of those who had ordered two desserts. Standing, she did not look so stalwart as she had sitting down. She had a wide but pleasant face and graying hair, and her figure, if considerable, was trim.

She said, "Farrell, Lucien," to the maître d'. She said, "Emily Farrell" to the others. "Mrs. Powers. Miss Farwell. Inspector Heimrich. Mrs. Heimrich. Miss Farwell. Miss Farwell is an author."

"Farrell," the stalwart woman with the pleasant face said. She spelled it out. "Of cookbooks," she said.

"Wait," Susan said. *"Emily Farrell's Gourmet Recipes.* You remember the beef in burgundy, Merton. It came out of her book. Marinated in cognac first."

"Perfectly," Heimrich said. "Delicious." His tone told Susan but no one else, she thought, that he did not remember it at all.

50

The maître d' still was standing. He looked at his watch again. He looked more anxiously around the room. Then he said, "Ah, the major," and took two steps down the room to meet the big and handsome youngish man with the clipped mustache who had sat with the Grimeses in the *veranda belvedere* and stayed on after them. He said, "Hope I'm not late, y'know."

He was Major Ian Whitney, or the maître d' thought he was. Whitney did not disagree, which, Susan thought, put the maître d' one up. Whitney repeated names as they were given him. He said, "Ah, Inspector. Heard of you, haven't I?" to Heimrich. To Mrs. Powers he said, "Evening, m'dear. Looking tops, y'know."

She said, "Thank you, Ian."

She smiled up at the youngish major. Her smile was not, Susan thought, noticeably cordial. It was noncommittal. I'm making up stories about people again, Susan thought. It's because of those weeks in the hospital, when it was too much trouble to read so I made up stories for myself.

Major Whitney sat down. The maître d' remained standing. He continued to look around the room. He maintained a welcoming smile, but that was, Susan thought, merely because he had forgotten to take it off. He looked at his watch. Susan looked at hers. It was still only a few minutes after seven. But it was after seven.

He made up his mind. He turned to his, apparently, inadequate flock. He said, "It appears the others have been delayed, signors, signoras. If you will follow me?"

They followed him. They followed above to the boat deck. They followed up another flight to the lido deck and forward on it, through a narrow corridor, and the maître d' knocked on a closed door, which was opened instantly by a steward in a stiff white jacket and black dress trousers.

The steward said, "Signors-signoras," and stepped aside out of the way of Comandante di Scarlotti, who wore a white mess jacket with shoulder boards and the four stripes of a captain and who was as tall as Merton Heimrich and Major Ian Whitney, who were very tall men and, for that matter, big men. Di Scarlotti was thinner, and a line of verse danced briefly in Susan's mind. "Clean favored and imperially slim." From—?

"Delighted," di Scarlotti said to Mrs. Powers, who was the first to go into the captain's suite when the maître d' stepped aside and bowed and motioned. "Delighted," to Susan. "Delighted," to Miss Emily Farrell. "Inspector. Major."

The comandante's "sitting room" was unexpectedly large. A cushioned bench ran along one wall—Bulkhead, Susan thought; I must remember—and there was a long, low table in front of it, with chairs clustered around the table. The steward who had let them in stood stiff and attentive. "Mrs. Powers?" Comandante di Scarlotti said. He had a low, easy voice. And, Susan thought, he has been briefed on names. Mrs. Powers would have a sherry; a quite dry sherry, if she might. "Mrs. Heimrich?"

The comandante's English was unaccented; the intonation was American. "What'll it be, Major?"

The Heimrichs asked for martinis; Merton was not as specific as usual, but he did ask the omission of an olive. Emily Farrell thought a dry sherry would be fine; Major Whitney asked for Scotch. "With just a splash of soda. No ice, if you don't mind?"

He's almost too English, Susan thought. Much more in his speech than Sir Ronald. Almost B.B.C., his speech is, although I suppose it's really one of the universities. The steward did not ask what the comandante wanted. That apparently went without saying—when he brought drinks on a silvery tray, Comandante di Scarlotti's was a small, pale sherry. While the drinks were being served nobody said anything, but the *Italia*'s captain smiled at all of them and, when all had drinks, lifted his glass and moved it in a circle which included all.

52

"Smooth crossing," Major Whitney said and then added, "what?"

"We're fortunate," the captain said. "Sometimes a little rough this early in the season."

A second steward brought canapés. Miss Farrell was the first to reach toward the tray when the steward put it in front of them. There was black caviar in a bowl of ice, and Miss Farrell reached for that. "And," she said, "you set a good table, Comandante." She smiled at him and nodded her head. He smiled back at her and said, "I understand you're an authority, Miss Farrell. Someone to please."

"You do," Emily Farrell said. "It's a fine boat, Captain."

He won't like "boat," Susan thought. It's odd Sir Ronald and Lady Grimes aren't at the party. A baronet ought to be very important. Probably there are parties like this every evening, and the Grimeses are being saved for another—a *very* V.I.P. party, probably.

Comandante di Scarlotti was glad they were making Miss Farrell comfortable.

This is going to be very stiff, Susan thought. I wish we were in Mario's bar. By ourselves. I wish—

Someone knocked at the door, and a steward opened it. The maître d' stepped aside. He said, "Mr. and Mrs. Primes, Comandante—I mean Sir Ronald and Lady Prime."

After all, Susan thought, he has to remember so many people. And I'm no good at names either. On the other hand, I'm not a maître d'.

Lady Grimes was very pretty indeed in a pale yellow dinner dress with a square-cut neckline. She wore earrings which were unobtrusive, considering they were obviously diamond earrings. She gets younger every time we see her, Susan thought. Tonight she's not a day over thirty.

Sir Ronald, on the other hand, did not grow younger. At first he had seemed too young, too quick and certain, to be of retirement age. Tonight he looked tired.

53

"Sorry, Captain." Grimes said. "Telephone call held me up. Evening, Mrs. Heimrich. Evening, Lucinda."

He smiled down at Mrs. Raymond Powers when he said, "Lucinda." He looked down at Emily Farrell and smiled, and di Scarlotti said, "Miss Farrell, Sir Ronald, Lady Grimes. An author."

"Not really," Miss Farrell said, "Just of cookbooks."

"Important things, cookbooks," Grimes said. "World lives by them, Miss Farrell. Or ought to. Heimrich. Whitney."

One of the stewards said, "Lady Grimes? Sir Ronald?"

"A martini," Ellen Grimes said. "Like those the Heimrichs are having."

Her husband, Susan thought, looked slightly surprised. He ordered Scotch and plain water. He didn't say anything about a "splash" of water. The steward said, "Ice, sir?" and Grimes said, "Yes, thank you."

"Sit here, won't you, Lady Grimes?" di Scarlotti said, and got up from his own chair, which was at one end of the oblong table. "Anywhere you like, Sir Ronald."

The three women were on the cushioned bench along the bulkhead, with Miss Farrell in the middle. Sir Ronald, with a choice open, sat next Susan Heimrich. Di Scarlotti went around the table and sat beside Mrs. Raymond Powers, who apparently was Lucinda Powers.

"We've spent a bit of time in the States," Ronald Grimes told Susan. "More than home, recent years. Picked up your habits, Mrs. Heimrich. Some of them. Ellen's martini, for example. Not so popular in England, y'know."

Ellen Grimes leaned a little toward them.

"Because," she said, "all our really good gin is exported. Mostly to the States, isn't it, Ronald? You'd know."

"Sort of commercial attaché at the Embassy," Grimes said. "What Ellen means by that. True enough, though. We get left with the seventy proof, y'know. Watery stuff. Explains the

54

gin-and-it people, probably. Pink-gin people too, I shouldn't wonder."

"We were down in Georgia a year or so ago," Ellen Grimes said. "Fed us bourbon whisky. With something called Six Up as a mixer. Very odd."

"Seven Up," Susan said, "I've never tried it."

"Very pleasant people in Georgia," Grimes said. "Ones we met, anyway."

"Oh," Ellen Grimes said, "very charming people. One or two of them did call me 'Mrs. Lady Grimes.'"

"Establishing our legitimacy," Grimes said. "See what I mean, Mrs. Heimrich?"

Susan smiled and nodded her head. The arrival of the Grimeses had, a little unexpectedly, moderated the stiffness of the party.

Lucinda Powers's voice cut into an instant of silence. It cut rather sharply. It was a higher voice than it had been. The steward had been bringing drinks, but Susan had shaken her head to offers. She still had much of her first martini. Mrs. Powers sounded—just barely sounded—as if she had not shaken her head. But, sherry? Susan looked at the glass in front of Lucinda Powers. It was a cocktail glass, not a sherry glass. The sherry glasses had been long-stemmed and fragile. The liquid in Mrs. Powers's glass was colorless. Not even the palest and driest of sherries is that colorless, Susan thought—which is none of my business.

"Wasn't he, Ronald?" Lucinda Powers said, in her heightened voice.

Grimes looked at her and said, "Sorry, Lucinda. Afraid I missed something."

"My late husband," Lucinda said. "My Ray. Everybody knew about him, didn't they?"

"Most people, certainly," Ronald Grimes said. "Very able man, your husband."

55

"More than that," Lucinda Powers said. "You know he was more than that, Ronald. A great man. A leader. You know that."

Ronald Grimes said, "Of course, Lucinda," but not, Susan thought, in a tone of great enthusiasm.

"Passed away just when he was most needed." Lucinda Powers said. "You know that, Ronald. You do too, Major."

"Captain-of-industry type," Major Whitney said. "Absolutely."

"And he worked himself to death," Lucinda Powers said. "For his country. Didn't he, Ronald?"

"You could call it that," Ronald Grimes said, and again Susan heard—thought she heard—a shade of withdrawal in his voice. "Entered into it, certainly."

"*You* know," Lucinda Powers said. "Nobody better. That's true, isn't it?"

She had taken over the conversation. Nobody else was saying anything. The party, Susan thought was no longer stiff. It was in danger of becoming strident, in a one-sided way. She looked across the table at her husband, but Merton was looking at Mrs. Powers, as the rest were looking at her. There was a noticeably withdrawn look on Comandante di Scarlotti's face, Susan thought.

"I knew your husband quite well, Lucinda," Grimes said. "A very forceful man. He—"

"Such excellent pâté, captain," Emily Farrell said. "Such a special flavor. Italian, isn't it?"

It was a try, Susan thought. Not much of a try, but something of a try. It was, she thought, much too early to leave the party. There was no good excuse to leave the party. Sometimes when a party begins to rasp you can say you have an early dinner date. It was not an excuse which would sound convincing on shipboard. On shipboard, people ate after the dinner chimes had sounded.

"Not forceful enough, was he, Ronald?" Mrs. Powers said. "Up against a wall at the Embassy, wasn't he? Your wall."

"Dear Lucinda," Ellen Grimes said, "there wasn't any wall, really. Just policy. Wasn't that it, Ronald?"

Sir Ronald said, "Absolutely. Great chap, Powers. Tops in his field. We all felt that, Lucinda."

"Carrying a bit of weight," Whitney said. "Puts a strain on the ticker, y'know."

His voice was level and, Susan thought, a little hard. Mrs. Powers looked at him, and her look was as hard as his voice. She said, "I wasn't talking to you, Major. You didn't know my husband."

"Oh," Whitney said, "ran into him here and there, m'dear. One place and another. Right, Ellen?"

"Dear boy," Ellen Grimes said. "How would I know whom you ran into here and there?"

"Sorry," Whitney said. "Wouldn't, of course. Don't know what made me say that, Lady Grimes."

The "Lady Grimes" had an edge to it, Susan thought. An edge of—what? Of satire? Of rebuke?

"Mrs. Lady Grimes," Emily Farrell said. "I think that's wonderful. I really think it's wonderful."

Ellen Grimes turned to Miss Farrell, and turned to her with a smile—a welcoming smile.

"Surprising, certainly," Ellen Grimes said. "Most—taking-abacking for a moment. But Ronald went out to Chicago once for—for a conference of some sort—and a reporter called him 'Sir Grimes.'"

She spoke rapidly, rather nervously. Accepting a diversion with eagerness, Susan thought; clutching at it with an anecdote not worth the telling.

"Unpolished," Susan said. "We crude Amuricans."

She spoke in the lightest of voices; a voice with laughter in it. She made much of the "u" in "Amuricans."

57

Ronald Grimes looked at her, and a wide smile split his tired face, and he said, "Jolly right, what-what?" burlesquing it. She smiled back at him, and then he turned to Major Whitney and said, "Eh, Whitney? Jolly good, wouldn't you say?"

With his head turned, Susan could no longer see the smile on Ronald Grimes's face. But she felt that, when he looked at the major, the smile wasn't there.

Major Whitney said, "Right you are, Grimes."

She could see his face, and there was no smile on it.

It's all very prickly, Susan thought. They're—they're talking behind their words.

"Leaving us at Málaga, I understand," Comandante di Scarlotti said. He said it to Merton Heimrich, who said, "Yes, Captain." There was quiet in Heimrich's voice. There was no edge on it. It is as if the tension has not reached him, Susan thought. As if it has escaped him. But things like that do not ever escape him.

"Tricky harbor, Málaga," di Scarlotti said. "Have to go in this way"—an index finger traced a line on the table in front of him. "Narrow. Crosscurrent. Then, around this way"—the finger traced "this way," which seemed to be a narrow circle. "And then"—the finger moved again.

"Looks confusing," Heimrich said.

"Can't say I like it too much," di Scarlotti said. "Tricky. Risk of putting her aground."

"But you never have," Heimrich said.

"Oh, no," the captain said. "Moments, you understand. But no, Inspector. Maneuverable ship, *Italia*. Handy ship. Steward?"

The steward was there. He said, "Sir?"

"Empty glasses," di Scarlotti said.

The hand which had been tracing a course into the harbor of Málaga traced a course over empty glasses. The steward said, "Sir," again and began to pick glasses up and put them on a tray. He took Merton Heimrich's glass, and Lucinda

58

Powers held hers out to him. But Ellen Grimes smiled and shook her head, and Susan put a hand over her half-empty glass. It was the hand with a watch on its wrist, and Susan saw that it was almost eight o'clock; time almost for the low-voiced chimes of dinner.

Whitney said, "Less soda, what? Said just a splash, y'know." His voice still was hard. He had, Susan thought, a singularly uninflected voice.

The steward said, "Sir."

"No ice," Whitney said, and the steward said, "Sir," again.

"Can't get used to the way you freeze your drinks," Whitney said, turned toward Heimrich. "Bad for the liver, eh?"

"Quite possibly," Heimrich said. "Our livers get used to it, I suppose. Learn to bear up."

"Room temperature doesn't mean the temperature of most rooms," Emily Farrell said. "The temperature of the cellar, actually. Isn't that right, Sir Ronald? Wines, I mean."

Grimes had been looking at his wife. He said, "Eh?" and then, "Sorry, Miss Farrell—?"

"The temperature of wines," she said. "Reds, of course. Cellar temperature, actually?"

"Oh, yes," Ronald Grimes said. "Quite right, Miss Farrell. When people had cellars, of course. Bit gone out now, I'm afraid. In my father's day. Grandfather's. Made a thing of it. Remember when I was just a young un my father—"

The chimes sounded. Sir Ronald's father faded with the chimes. Sir Ronald stopped speaking and looked across the table at his wife.

"Yes, dear," Ellen Grimes said. "I do think so." She offered a smile around. "He does get so hungry on sea voyages," she said. "Ravenous, really. But it doesn't seem to do anything for him. I mean, ten stone. Tall as he is. And people are supposed to gain weight when they quit smoking."

She's nervous, Susan thought. It's nervousness talking.

Lady Grimes began to stand up. The men seemed to

59

bounce to their feet, and Comandante di Scarlotti was first to stand. As a host should be, Susan thought. But he's glad his party's over. Because it was—what do they say of harbor water? Choppy. It was a choppy party. With undercurrents. With meanings below the surface of words.

She stood with the others. With the others she said, "Delightful party, Comandante," and with the others went out of the comandante's sitting room.

Di Scarlotti went with them. It was a little, Susan thought, as if he were a country host seeing his guests to their cars. He did not see them to either of the nearby elevators; he saw them down the stairs from deck to deck and, although the ship was moving perceptibly, he did not touch a handrail. Susan Heimrich slid a hand down a rail, but Merton Heimrich, walking down beside her, was as sure-footed, as unconcerned by the ship's movement, as the ship's captain.

Mrs. Powers clung to a rail, and to it for only one flight down. Then she left them and stood, swaying with the ship, in front of the sign which read "Ascensore."

Miss Emily Farrell started down the first flight in its center, out of reach of the rails on either side. But she swayed with the ship, or a little more than the ship swayed, and Merton Heimrich took her arm gently and pulled her within reach of the rail.

"Such a lovely party, wasn't it," Emily Farrell said. "I do wish I knew what made the pâté so special."

Sir Ronald and Lady Grimes had no trouble with the ship's movement, but she held his arm. Major Ian Whitney practically tripped down the stairs. Probably, Susan thought, he takes a cold tub every morning and jogs all day. I shouldn't be surprised if he rides to hounds, too.

After dinner—and another half bottle of Soave Bolla— they went up to the *salone delle feste*, which translated "ballroom." It was Merton Heimrich's suggestion. "We're all dressed up," he said. "You shimmer. I want to show you off.

We might even dance, if you don't mind dancing with a hip—"

Her smiling look, her shaken head, stopped him. They went by elevator to the promenade deck and forward to the ballroom. It was almost filled, but a captain of stewards found them a table. The table was close to the dance floor, on which there was no dancing—on which cardboard horses with numbers on them were arranged on squares. They were in a single line, so the race was just beginning. A steward came to their table. "Signor, signora, you would care to place a bet?"

They bought tickets at two dollars each, selecting their numbers. Susan's was 2; Heimrich's 4. A man at a microphone on a stage by the dance floor said, "Ladies and gentlemen. The first race will be a steeplechase. When you have made your bets?"

There was a pause, and everybody looked at the slender young man at the microphone. He said, "Signors, signoras," in an approving voice. He said, "Guido?"

It was their Guido. They must make them work very hard, Susan thought. Guido brought a dice box to their table. He put it down in front of Susan and said, "Signora Heimrich? If you will?"

Susan shook the box and spilled two dice from it. She threw a double six. Guido turned toward the man at the microphone and raised his voice and said, "Six, signor. And six."

The Number 6 horse was moved forward two squares. Heimrich raised a hand to a waiter and said to Susan, "You threw the boxcars, darling." She raised her shoulders in inquiry, and Heimrich said, to the waiter, "Two Martel cognac, please. Not in snifters." The waiter said, "Sir."

When he had gone, Susan said, "Boxcars?"

"Because they look like them," Merton said, and Susan said, "Of course, the dice."

"Yes," Merton said. "When I was a young trooper, there was a suicide in my district. A very wealthy one. One worth

61

press coverage. A reporter phoned his story in. He said, 'Old Nelson—Jonathan J. Nelson—just threw the boxcars.' He meant Nelson had killed himself."

Susan said she didn't get it. Merton was not sure he did. He thought it might be the reporter's special argot. He said, "In a crap game, throw a double six and you're out. I suppose that was it. But why suicide I don't know. Bad luck is more what it sounds like."

Susan said, "Hmmm," and looked around the room. On the other side of the dance floor, Sir Ronald and Lady Grimes were sitting at a table for four. Lucinda Powers and Emily Farrell were sitting with them. Miss Farrell was eating canapés from a tray in the center of their table.

"They're continuing the party," Susan said. "Only it seemed to me that the Grimeses and Mrs. Powers didn't quite—"

She did not finish, because Heimrich's nod had finished for her.

"Three, signor," Guido said, from across the room. "And a deuce."

Horses 2 and 3 were each advanced a square, but Horse Number 6 remained ahead.

Their cognacs came, not in snifters. They also got a small plate of canapés.

"At this rate," Susan said, "I'll begin to weigh in stones too."

But she took a canapé to go with a sip from her glass. "One, signor," Guido called from another part of the spreading room. "And a three."

Horses advanced. Horse 3 was now even with Horse 6.

"At least," Susan said, "Mine's started. Yours just stands there."

"You jinxed him," Merton said. "You and your boxcars."

"Six," Guido called. "And an ace."

A rather heavy woman in a pinkish dinner dress went to the Grimeses' table and smiled down at those sitting there.

And Sir Ronald stood up, and the women stood up. Ellen Grimes said something to her husband, and he smiled at her and his lips moved. Susan thought he had said, "Of course, darling." But Susan cannot read lips. She was merely supplying dialogue to go with action.

The action was that the four women threaded their way among tables and out of the ballroom, and that Ronald Grimes sat down again and finished his tall drink.

But he finished it in only a minute or two. Then he stood up and went across the room toward an exit, which was not the one the women had taken.

Detective Inspector Albert Hunt got up out of nowhere, which was apparently where he lived, and went out after Grimes.

"And double six," Guido said, from a far side of the big room.

"What it is," Susan said, as Horse Number 6 went forward two squares, "the dice are fixed. Your poor Number Four."

Horse Number 4, which was a rather drab brown-pink horse, still stood at the starting gate. Number 2 was only one square down the course. Number 6 was a square from the finish line. And the big room had begun to fill with voices. Susan finished her small cognac, making rather a point of it. Merton said, "Yes, I think so. There are going to be six more races before the dancing starts."

"Deuce," Guido said. "And four."

"At last," Susan said, and began to stand up. "While our luck is in."

Heimrich put "Cab. 82" on the bar check, and they went out of the room. When he pressed a button for the elevator, its doors opened immediately. "Waiting for us," Susan said, and went into the elevator.

When Heimrich reached toward the button marked "PS," Susan said, "No, I want to see something," and pressed the button which was marked "PLa." So they went above instead of below, and Heimrich raised both his shoulders and his eyebrows. He said, "Mario? After cognac?"

"Curiosity," Susan said, and the door opened, and they went out into the foyer of the boat deck.

Susan led them through the starboard passageway, which took them past the open doorway of the card room.

There were three tables of bridge, and Ellen Grimes and Lucinda Powers and Emily Farrell were at one of them, with the woman in the pinkish dinner dress. Mrs. Powers and Lady Grimes were partners.

"Four no trump," Lucinda Powers said, with much firmness in her voice. The woman in the pinkish dress said, "Pass." Lady Grimes looked at her cards.

They could not stand outside the card-room door and stare. They went on into the *veranda belvedere*, which was almost deserted. Which was not quite deserted. Sir Ronald Grimes and Detective Inspector Hunt were sitting together in what would have been a corner, if the room had had corners. A steward was leaning down toward them, his pad ready. Not Mario, who must be off duty at this hour.

Susan and Merton Heimrich went out of the room through the passageway to port.

The doors to the library and writing room were open, but the rooms were empty.

As they waited for the elevator, Susan said, "I thought the woman in the awful pink dress was the fourth for bridge. I just wanted—"

The elevator door opened, and they got in. This time Merton pressed the "PS" button, and no objection was entered, and the elevator started down toward the *ponte superiore*, where their cabin was.

"I do hope they'd established their suit," Susan said, as they walked toward Cabin 82. "I hate that four-no-trump bid. It's so—so commanding. And the back of Ellen Grimes's head looked worried."

ꭡ 5

S.S. *Italia* still moved easily that fourth morning
out. Her bow rose a little and dipped a little. From their chairs
on the promenade deck they could see the Atlantic, and the
Atlantic was a calm ocean. By raising himself a little in his
chair, Heimrich could see the froth of the bow wave. The sliding glass panels were farther open this morning at a little after
ten. The air which came through them was soft air.

"We've sailed away from winter," Susan said.

Merton Heimrich said, "Hmmm."

"We should go up to the boat deck and walk around the
ship, breathing deeply," Susan said. "We should bestir ourselves."

Her husband said, "Hmmm," again. "Hmmm" expressed
agreement. It did not indicate imminent action.

Behind them there were sounds—a thud of something
heavy being put down on the deck; the faint chipping sound
of china.

"But we just had breakfast," Susan said. "They're setting
up for consommé."

Heimrich said, "Hmmm."

"You sound," she told him, "as if you were going to sleep."

He brought himself to words. He said, "Not quite."

"Not," she said, "that it isn't fine for you. This is being good for you. No murderers."

It is Heimrich's job to catch murderers. He said, "Hmmm," and the sound was one of contentment. He closed his eyes. It was, of course, absurd to feel drowsy at a little after ten in the morning, after a long night's sleep. It was—

"Inspector Heimrich?"

He opened his eyes. He looked up at a young ship's officer, who stood very erect in a white uniform with a single stripe on each of his shoulder-boards. He said, "Signor Inspector?"

Heimrich said, "Yes?"

"The captain's compliments, sir," the younger officer said. "The captain would appreciate it if you could spare him a few minutes in his quarters, sir. Comandante di Scarlotti, Inspector, sir."

Heimrich raised his eyebrows.

"He would very much appreciate it, signor," the officer said. "In his quarters, sir. There has been a—an incident, sir."

Heimrich put one foot down on the deck. He followed it with the other foot. He turned to Susan and looked down at her, his eyebrows arched.

"Perhaps," Susan said, "Horse Number Four really won. At tremendous odds. You are supposed to cash in your ticket."

He smiled faintly as he stood up.

"No," Susan said, "I don't believe it either." Then she said, "And it was so peaceful."

Heimrich stood up.

"I'll be here," Susan said, "Drinking consommé. Or, you'll find me. I won't get off the ship."

Heimrich followed the young officer through a door and up two flights of stairs to the lido deck and forward to the comandante's quarters. A steward opened the door to the sitting room. Di Scarlotti was sitting at the table around which they had sat the evening before. He had a coffee cup in his hand. He put it down when Heimrich went into the sitting room and stood up. He looked worried, Heimrich thought. He looked a good deal worried.

"Good morning, Inspector," di Scarlotti said. "I am sorry to have disturbed you. Mrs. Heimrich? She is well this morning? There was some motion during the night. She—you—were not inconvenienced?"

"We were fine," Heimrich said. "And it is quite calm this morning."

"The water, yes," di Scarlotti said. "There is no sea running. A light swell only. You will have coffee, Inspector?" He did not wait for an answer. He said, "Coffee for the inspector, steward." He motioned toward the chair next his own. Heimrich sat in it. The steward brought coffee. He said, "Sir?" to Comandante di Scarlotti. Di Scarlotti said, "*Grazie*," and continued in Italian. The steward said, "Signor," and went out of the sitting room.

"I am most sorry to have disturbed you," di Scarlotti said. "Something has occurred. Something most unfortunate. I—since you are in my ship—I—but it is more than I should ask. That I realize, Inspector. But you are a police official. Have experience in such matters."

"A police officer," Heimrich said. "A cop, Comandante. What matters?"

Comandante di Scarlotti lifted his coffee cup and shook his head at it and put it down again. He said, "It is most unfortunate, Inspector. It is a matter of great concern."

It occurred to Heimrich that di Scarlotti had learned English overabundantly. He looked at the man with the surprisingly deep blue eyes, who sat so erect in his chair—and who was so worried and was taking so many words to tell what worried him. His intonation was less American, his sentences

67

more formal than in the easy atmosphere of his cocktail party. Only last night in these same quarters.

"Sir Ronald," di Scarlotti said. "Sir Ronald Grimes. He has—he seems to have disappeared, Inspector. We fear—Comandante Ferrancci and I both fear—that there has been an accident. But—" He did not immediately go on. He looked at Heimrich, and it seemed to Heimrich that there was a question in his very blue eyes. Heimrich waited.

"The sea has been calm," di Scarlotti said. "Last night only a little sea. But even in rough weather *Italia* is a steady ship. And the rails to which passengers have access—well, they are high, Inspector."

"Yes," Heimrich said. "You think Sir Ronald has fallen overboard? Is that it, Captain?"

"But it would be very difficult," di Scarlotti said. "It has never happened before, Inspector."

"You've had the ship searched?" Heimrich said.

Di Scarlotti's hands moved. They seemed to brush away the obvious. He said, "Certainly, Inspector. We have a security force which is excellent. It is under Comandante Ferrancci. He supervises the crew, you will understand. He is qualified to command, of course. He is the—what is the term in English?"

"Staff captain?" Heimrich said.

Di Scarlotti said, "Sì, Inspector."

"All classes? The crew's quarters? A man could go from one class to another? I mean, there aren't locked doors or anything?"

"Only notices. 'First Class,' 'Cabin,' 'Tourist.' In Italian and English. There are no locked doors. That—that would not be safe, Inspector. Yes, my security men have searched everywhere. Sir Ronald is not—I greatly fear, Inspector, that Sir Ronald is not aboard the ship. He is an important man, Inspector. At least, that is what I've been told. We are, as you would say, briefed about the passengers. By the head office."

By the public relations office, Heimrich assumed. Which would account for the selected cocktail party in the sitting room.

"What you're getting at," Heimrich said, "what you're afraid of—he may have been pushed overboard. Lifted over the rail and—and dropped."

"It would be most unfortunate," di Scarlotti said. "It—it would reflect on the line, Inspector. And on me, as captain of the *Italia*. As responsible for her safety. And the safety of those in her. He was an important man, Inspector."

"Also," Heimrich said, "he was a light man. For his height. Lady Grimes said ten stone last night. A hundred and forty pounds. Very little weight for his height."

"And," di Scarlotti said, "he was not a young man, Inspector."

"Appeared to be fit enough," Heimrich said. "But—no, not young. The ship rolled somewhat during the night?"

"A little. The stabilizers are most effective. But, a little."

"A strong person," Heimrich said, "standing behind Grimes, say. Taking advantage of the ship's movement? That's what you're afraid of?"

"What has been in my mind," di Scarlotti said. "Most uneasily in my mind, Inspector."

"Why?"

Di Scarlotti looked at him a little blankly. He repeated the word "why."

"Sir Ronald was, I assume, on a list of passengers due special attention," Heimrich said. "As my wife and I apparently were. The point is, had you known Sir Ronald before last night, Captain? Have any special reason to think somebody might—well, have pushed him over the side?"

"I did not know him. I had been—told about him. There was a memo. A man with a distinguished career in the British foreign service. And a baronet. The eighth baronet, I think. Perhaps the seventh. And—"

69

"Yes," Heimrich said. "And I suppose you got a memo about me, Captain. That catching murderers is my trade? Did the memo also say that I'm on leave, Captain? That my wife has been ill? That we are on holiday? And, of course, that I have no authority on your ship?"

"I did not know about your wife, Inspector. I am most sorry. That you are a celebrated detective. Yes. I was informed of that."

"And," Heimrich said, "decided I was handy." There was no use arguing about the word "celebrated."

The comandante of S.S. *Italia* smiled faintly.

"That you are experienced in such matters," di Scarlotti said. "That you might give us the benefit of your experience. As for authority, Inspector, the master of a ship at sea has considerable—latitude."

Heimrich drank from his coffee cup. Di Scarlotti pushed a pack of cigarettes—American cigarettes—within reach, and Heimrich shook a cigarette out of it. He accepted a light from di Scarlotti. But then he shook his head.

"There's a man aboard who could be of much more help," he said. "He's also a police officer. A detective inspector. British. Scotland Yard, for all I know. And, he knows—knew may be the word—Sir Ronald. They had some contact in London a while back. Sir Ronald mentioned it. No details. Last night they were having drinks together in the observation lounge. If what you're afraid of is true, he's your man, Captain. Albert Hunt, his name is. Detective Inspector. Not on your briefing list, apparently."

"No," di Scarlotti said. "I had not heard of him. He knew Sir Ronald, you say?"

"Well enough so that the Grimes called him 'Bert,' " Heimrich said. "That they had drinks together. And—seemed to have a good deal to say to each other."

"That was last night, you say?"

"Last night. Oh—no later than half past ten. In the observation lounge."

Di Scarlotti said, "Ah." He got up and crossed the room to a desk and picked up a telephone. He said, "Purser, please." Almost at once he said, "Morning." Then he continued in Italian. The name "Hunt" stuck out of the Italian.

He put the telephone back in its cradle.

"Cabin One-oh-eight," he said. "Not far from your own, Inspector. He will be asked to join us."

The "us" stuck out a little. Heimrich pushed back his chair.

"If you will wait, Inspector?" di Scarlotti said. "I would appreciate it if you would wait. You have met Inspector Hunt?"

"Introduced to him," Heimrich said. "No real—"

He did not finish. There was nothing tangible. But Hunt had looked across rooms at him; had once or twice moved as if he thought of crossing rooms to speak to a man in the same line of work. It was no more than that, of course. Still—

Heimrich sat down again. He said, "When did you hear that Sir Ronald was missing, Captain?"

"Quite early this morning," di Scarlotti said. "Lady Grimes discovered he was not in his cabin. And that his bed had not been slept in. She was—disturbed. The steward and the stewardess, they had not seen Sir Ronald. So—" He spread his hands. "So we began the search," he said.

"The Grimeses had separate cabins? You said 'his' cabin."

"Cabins Sixteen and Eighteen," di Scarlotti said. "A suite. Connecting cabins, of course. On the *ponte lance*, Inspector. The boat deck."

"The open promenade," Heimrich said. "The one with the rail around it?"

"Yes. The rail is most substantial, Inspector. And quite high."

"Lady Grimes hadn't waited up for her husband?" Heimrich said. "Just assumed he had gone to his cabin and gone to bed? Or had she seen him earlier when he came in?"

"Apparently not," di Scarlotti said. "She had, she says, been playing bridge until quite late. After midnight, she thinks—"

Sir Ronald and Lady Grimes had, after dinner, gone up to

71

the ballroom. "There was horse racing. Afterward, dancing." Miss Emily Farrell and Mrs. Powers had joined them for a drink. Bridge had been arranged—Lady Grimes, Miss Farrell, Mrs. Powers and a Mrs. Peterson. (Mrs. Peterson, Heimrich gathered, had not been listed as a V.I.P. on the captain's memo.) Mrs. Peterson was a little late in joining the others. When she came the women went to the card room. Sir Ronald remained at the table. He—

"I know," Heimrich said. "We saw them. Finished his drink and went out. Alone, but I think Inspector Hunt went out at about the same time."

"You were there?" di Scarlotti said.

"For a time," Heimrich said. "Our horses were more or less left at the starting gate. It must have been—oh, a little after ten when Lady Grimes and her friends went out. My wife and I happened to go past the card room later on and looked in. They were playing bridge. And Sir Ronald and Hunt were at a table in the observation lounge, and a steward was taking their drink orders. You go past the card room to get to the observation lounge, as I remember. Can, anyway. Lady Grimes didn't see her husband then? I mean when he and Hunt—together or one at a time—went into the lounge?"

"Not after she left him in the ballroom," di Scarlotti said. "They may have gone in through the port passageway, of course."

It was taking Detective Inspector Hunt a time, Heimrich thought. A late riser, perhaps. In the middle of breakfast. Or, naturally, taking a turn around the deck. And since it would be Hunt who would cooperate with *Italia*'s security force, if anybody did—

But Inspector Heimrich did not again push back his chair.

"Some time after midnight," Heimrich said, "they finished bridge. Lady Grimes went back to the cabins. On the same deck. But through the ship, I suppose? I mean, she didn't go out on the deck?"

"The cabins do not open from the outer deck, Inspector. From a passageway."

"Went into her own cabin. Which one was it, Captain?"

"Eighteen, I believe. It is the larger of the two."

"The door to her husband's cabin was closed? At least, I assume it was. She'd have looked in otherwise and seen he wasn't there."

"I do not know, Inspector. Probably you are right. But—Lady Grimes is much disturbed, you will understand. A stewardess is with her. And a doctor. It is not the time to—to press her for such details."

And I'm not the one to do the pressing, Heimrich thought. Up to Hunt, if he wants to take it on. Or one of the ship's security men. Time Hunt got along. When he did, he would have to go over the same ground Heimrich himself was going over—going over to no purpose, naturally, since if it was a case it would be Hunt's case. But curiosity about murder, if all of this was actually about murder, is habit-forming.

"Cabins Sixteen and Eighteen form a suite, you say," Heimrich said. "I take it there is a connecting door?"

"Yes. Certainly."

"Lady Grimes happen to say whether it was open when she went into her cabin?"

"She is much disturbed. As is natural, of course. We—we have tried to intrude as little as possible. I do not know if she has been asked about the door between the cabins."

"Probably closed," Heimrich said. "Otherwise she'd have —oh, called through or something, naturally. Or looked in to say good night."

"It was quite late," di Scarlotti said. "She assumed he had gone to bed and was asleep. She had summoned her steward to order breakfast. Had ordered for both of them. When the steward and stewardess brought the breakfasts, the door between the rooms was closed. Lady Grimes knocked on it,

73

and there was no answer. She called through—the steward and stewardess were arranging the trays at the time. She opened the door, finally. The room was empty. The bed was undisturbed. She—she asked the steward to see whether Sir Ronald was in his bathroom. He was not, of course."

Heimrich wondered what terms Sir Ronald and Lady Grimes were on—or had been on. Seeing them together, he had thought them close, quickly responsive to each other. But an outsider cannot tell. And I am an outsider to all this, Heimrich thought. It is no affair of mine. And where the hell is Detective Inspector Albert Hunt?

"Have your men finished searching the ship, Captain?" Heimrich asked. "It is quite a large ship. You've been at it since—?"

"A little after eight," di Scarlotti said. "Yes, my men are still looking, of course. There are many places he might be, I suppose. Not places one would expect him to be, but—"

Di Scarlotti shrugged his shoulders and spread his hands. He had expressive shoulders and expressive hands.

Heimrich looked at his watch. It was a quarter of eleven. More than two hours they had been looking. And they would know where to look. He said, "The crew's quarters, of course?" and di Scarlotti said, "Yes." He added, "Everywhere, Inspector."

"The public rooms, naturally. Other cabins?"

"Passengers are being asked, Inspector. We cannot, as you would put it, simply barge in."

Heimrich nodded his head in understanding. He looked at his watch again and again wondered what the hell was holding Hunt to what was, by now, an obvious dawdle. They would be serving consommé on the promenade deck at any moment. Susan would be wondering what was keeping him. She would, he thought, be making up stories to fit the situation. And she would begin to worry. He did not want her to worry. And there was no real reason for his staying here, asking questions

Hunt, if Hunt decided to help the ship's captain, would have to ask over again.

Heimrich said, "We-ll," and pushed his chair back again from the table, and somebody knocked at the door. At last Detective Inspector Albert Hunt, answering a plea for—

The steward appeared out of an adjoining room of the captain's quarters. He opened the door.

It was not Detective Inspector Hunt standing outside the door. It was the young officer who had guided Heimrich to the captain's sitting room. The man behind him was not Hunt either. The man behind him was Guido—Guido the steward, grave and unhappy.

"Sir," the young officer said, "I am afraid something—that something has happened to Signor Hunt."

Di Scarlotti looked at the officer. He said, "Happened to him?"

"Sir," the officer said. "I am afraid—it appears that Signor Hunt is dead, Comandante. Guido here—tell him, Guido."

"Come inside and close the door," di Scarlotti said. They came inside and Guido closed the door after them.

"The purser called Signor Hunt on the telephone," the officer said. "He did not answer. I went to deliver your message, sir. But Guido—tell him, Guido."

"At eight he usually rang for us," Guido said. "For me, sir. To bring breakfast. Each morning, but not this morning. We do not disturb the passengers until they are ready, sir. But I had been in the passageway. He had not gone below for breakfast. I would have seen him."

Di Scarlotti spoke rapidly in Italian. Guido started to answer in Italian.

"In English, man," di Scarlotti said. "So that the inspector can understand you."

"I heard his telephone ringing, sir," Guido said. "It kept on ringing. But I was certain he was in his cabin, sir. So—"

So Guido knocked on the door of Hunt's cabin, and when

75

nothing had come of that had opened the door and said, "Good morning, signor. Did you ring for me, signor?"

There had been no answer, and the steward had gone on into the cabin.

Hunt was in his bed. He was not lying comfortably in his bed. He was twisted in it, and one foot was on the floor. And he was clothed, except that the collar of his soft dress shirt was open, and his black tie was on the deck beside the bed.

Guido said, "Signor? *Signor!*" and had realized there was no good in that and had put a hand on Hunt's forehead. But by then he had seen enough for that to be unnecessary.

"He was cold, sir," Guido said. "There were marks on his throat. I was on the telephone, calling for the doctor, when the signor came."

Guido's hands identified the signor as the young officer.

A doctor had come up from the *infermeria* on A deck. He had come quickly, but there had been no use in hurrying.

Detective Inspector Albert Hunt had been dead for at least six hours. He had been strangled—manually strangled, from the appearance of his throat. It appeared that he had struggled, but only briefly. Pressure on the carotid artery, the doctor thought. Such pressure can end life quickly.

"The body is still there?" Heimrich asked, and his voice was, suddenly, a policeman's voice.

The young officer loooed surprised. He said, "But no, Signor Inspector. Signor Hunt was dead, Inspector. His body was taken to the *infermeria*. For further examination, the doctor said."

Inspector M. L. Heimrich, New York State Police, said, "Damn!" He said, "Photographed?"

The young officer said, "Signor Inspector?"

"The body," Heimrich said. "Did anybody take pictures of it? Before it was moved?"

The officer looked at Guido, and both of them shook their heads.

"But no, Signor Inspector," the officer said. "He was not —it was not a thing to be looked at. His face—it was not a face one would want a picture of."

Heimrich thought Damn! again, but there was no point in saying it.

"You want more, Inspector?" Comandante di Scarlotti said.

Heimrich wanted a good deal more. There was no point in saying that, either.

"I'll look at the body later," he said. "After they have examined it."

And he knew that he had committed himself. But Hunt had been a policeman, too. People cannot be allowed to get away with killing policemen.

The young officer said, "Sir?" to the ship's master.

"Yes," di Scarlotti said. "You may go. If the inspector wishes to question you further he will—?" He looked at Heimrich, who said, "Yes. Nothing more for now."

The young officer and Guido went out of the captain's quarters. Di Scarlotti said, "Inspector Heimrich?"

"Yes," Heimrich said. "What I can do, naturally."

"I am—I shall be most grateful," di Scarlotti said. "It is fortunate that you are aboard, Inspector."

Heimrich said, "Hmmm." He said, "I'm afraid your men won't find Sir Ronald, Captain. Have them go on looking, of course. But I don't think they'll find him. I think Inspector Hunt saw him killed, don't you, Captain? Or could guess who killed him?"

⚓ 6

"We're on *holiday*," Susan said when he told her. But there was resignation in her voice, not resentment. Then she said, "I liked Sir Ronald. And poor Ellen Grimes. They—I think they were very close, Merton."

"I think so," Merton Heimrich said. "And Hunt was a cop, of course. It—well, that makes a difference. I'm hooked, Susan. It's a damn nuisance, but I'm hooked."

He had sat down in the chair next Susan's on the promenade deck. He started to get up.

"And it was being such a lovely holiday," Susan said.

He leaned down and kissed her. It didn't matter a damn that there were other people around.

"We'll save what we can of it," Heimrich said. "Anyway, I won't have to be off at the other end of somewhere when dinner's ready."

Susan agreed that there was that. Heimrich looked at his watch. It was eleven-thirty.

"The *veranda belvedere* in about an hour?" he said, and she said, "Yes. dear. And I'll tell Mario what we want, so you'll be on time."

Heimrich went through a door and down a passageway. He

78

knocked on the door of Cabin 18, which was amidships. A stewardess opened it and said, "Signor?"

Heimrich said his name. He said he would like to see Lady Grimes for a few minutes.

"I do not know," the stewardess said. "The signora is resting. She is not well, the poor lady. I do not think—"

Lady Ellen Grimes spoke from within the room. She said, "Ask Inspector Heimrich to come in, please."

The cabin was considerably larger than Cabin 82. It was large enough for a sofa under one of the windows with a small table in front of it, and two chairs opposite the sofa. The bed was farther along in a line with the sofa, under the other window. Lady Grimes was sitting on the sofa. She was dressed in a suit, as if to go somewhere. Her face was drawn. She looked up quickly when Heimrich went into the room, but she did not see in his face what, clearly, she had hoped to see.

"They haven't," she said, and her voice, which had had gaiety in it the evening before, was dulled.

"No," Heimrich said. "I'm sorry, Lady Grimes. They're—they're still searching the ship. Feel up to talking to me? The captain's asked me to lend a hand."

"Because they think—you all think—Ronald's dead. Isn't that it, Inspector?"

"We don't know," Heimrich said and sat down in one of the chairs facing Ellen Grimes. "They are still searching the ship. He may—is his health good, Lady Grimes?"

"You think a—a heart attack? Something like that? And that he may have—fallen down somewhere. May be lying somewhere unconscious?"

"There's always a chance of that," Heimrich said.

"No," she said. "At least, so far as I know he was well. He had no—no real difficulties with his health." She looked at Heimrich very intently. She said, "He's dead, isn't he, Inspector?"

"We don't—"

79

"Isn't he?"

There was really nothing for it.

"I'm afraid so," Heimrich said. "You see, something else has happened. Something about which there isn't any doubt, I'm sorry to say. You knew Inspector Hunt, Lady Grimes? You and Sir Ronald knew him?"

"Ronald did. I—oh, I'd met him. There was something, a long time ago I think, in London, that he and my husband did something about. Did it together. I don't know anything more about it. He is—I think what they call 'Special Branch.' Hush-hush things, I think. Why do you ask about him, Inspector? When my husband—"

Suddenly she put her hands up and hid her face behind them. She merely waited then, her face hidden.

"Inspector Hunt has been killed, Lady Grimes. Because— I'm afraid because he knew something about Sir Ronald's disappearance. Somebody got into his cabin some time last night and strangled him." He paused. "The captain—Comandante di Scarlotti—has asked me to help. Because I'm a policeman."

She took her hands down. She said. "But he seemed to be —oh, I don't know—such a harmless little man."

"Not to somebody," Heimrich said. "He may—well, have seen something."

"What you mean is, somebody killing Ronald. That's what you mean, isn't it?"

"I don't know. Yes, it could have been."

"How? I mean, you think somebody killed my husband. I can see that. How?"

"I don't know. It's possible—well, it's possible he was pushed over the side. Perhaps—oh, knocked unconscious first. I'm only guessing."

She covered her face again. Heimrich could see the shudder which ran through her slim body. She took her hands down. She said, "If somebody did—did such a dreadful thing —you'll find him, won't you? You will, won't you?"

"Try," Heimrich said. "I know it's hard to talk about it,

Lady Grimes. But will you tell me something about your husband. And about last night?"

"He was a good man. A—a dear man. Dear to me—very dear to me. He was retired, you know. They have to retire early in his service. He was only sixty. We—we were going to live in the manor house and grow flowers." She broke off. "And grow flowers," she repeated. "What can I tell you about last night, Inspector?"

"When you saw him last. What happened. Where you were."

She said, "Of course," and her voice, which had been shaken before, was steady. She told him. It was what she had told before and had been relayed to Heimrich by the ship's captain. Yes, the door into his cabin from the passageway had been closed. Yes, the door from her cabin to his had been closed. She had not seen Ronald and Detective Inspector Hunt walk past the card room toward the observation lounge. Or away from it. She had been sitting with her back to the door. Sometimes Sir Ronald had wanted to go to bed early. When he did, he closed the door to his room. "It was the same when we lived in Washington." It did not mean anything except that he wanted to sleep. Last night she had assumed that he had gone to bed early. "He never cared much for bridge. He had to play sometimes, of course. And he was a good player. But he didn't really—"

She stopped suddenly. She said, "I'm not usually like this. Don't twitter like this. It doesn't matter whether he liked to play bridge, does it?"

"Somebody may have known that," Heimrich said. "That he wouldn't be playing cards. Did he walk on the deck much, Lady Grimes? The open deck?"

"The Englishman keeping fit? No. He wasn't like that. People like that amused him."

"Tell me more about him. I—you'll see I have to ask these things, Lady Grimes."

"He was the eighth baronet. He had been in the foreign

81

service for years. Years before I met him. Most of the time since we've been married he's been at the U.N. Or, recently, at the Embassy. We've been in Washington—oh. it must be five years. He was—the commercial attaché. Something like that. He said he was, really, a glorified salesman. For our products in the States. It was his way of putting it."

"You've been married how long, Lady Grimes?"

"Eight years. Yes, I'm much younger than he—he was. More than twenty years younger. Were you going to ask that?"

"No. Oh, anything you want to tell me, Lady Grimes."

"It wasn't because I wanted to be Lady Grimes," she said. "It wasn't anything like that. Did you think it was something like that?"

"No."

"He was older, yes. And there is a lot of money. We got married because we loved each other."

Her body was shaking again. She was losing control, a little, of her body and of her words.

"My people are county," she said. "It doesn't mean anything. I know that. But—but—"

He waited and could see her steady.

"I'm being absurd," she said. "This has nothing to do with anything. Probably you don't even know what I mean by county.'"

"Yes," Heimrich said. "I know what you mean." Suddenly he smiled. "In a way," he said, "not precisely the English way, my wife's county too. Her people lived in the same place for a good many generations. In the same house. I'm—well, I'm just what we call a farm boy."

Not a cop asking questions. An acquaintance filling in a background. Oh, a cop asking questions. Seeking relaxation in the one questioned. Perhaps it was working. She wasn't shaking any more. She was still in shock. Probably she'd be in shock for a long time.

"Ronald was married before I knew him," she said. "His first wife died. They had a son. He'll be the ninth baronet. Is—is he now, Inspector? Is he already the ninth baronet? Sir Michael Grimes, Bart?"

Heimrich closed his eyes and waited.

"Leftenant Sir Michael Grimes, Bart," she said. "He's a fine boy, Inspector. He went to Sandhurst. All the Grimeses did. Except Ronald. He went to Oxford and then into the foreign service and—"

And her hands went up again to hide her strained face. But it was, he thought, doing her good to talk. At least, it wasn't doing her harm to talk.

"My wife was married before," Heimrich said. "To a man who was killed in Korea. They had a son—my son now in all that matters. His name is Michael too, Lady Grimes. Michael Faye his name is. He's a fine boy too."

"It's strange," she said. "Strange the way things happen, isn't it?"

It was not clear what was strange. Perhaps that they both had stepsons named Michael. Which was not really especially strange.

"Should I send him a wireless, Inspector? He's stationed at Gib just now. Tell him—tell him he's Sir Michael Gimes, ninth baronet?"

"We're not certain of that," Heimrich said. "But—yes, I suppose you'll want to tell him something. Is there—are there others to tell?"

"My people," she said. "There aren't any more Grimeses except Michael. No close ones, anyway. And—I suppose the Foreign Office?"

"I'll take care of that," Heimrich said. "Or, Comandante di Scarlotti will."

"There's Ian," she said. "Major Whitney. He's a military attaché at the Embassy in Washington. On leave. He—he could —could send a report through."

Heimrich shook his head.

"I'd rather," he said, "that as few people as possible know what's happened. What we're afraid has happened. Until—

well, until we're more certain what *has* happened."

"Will we ever be?"

It was a point, certainly. It was unlikely they would ever find a body to make it a certainty.

"Yes," Heimrich said. "We'll find out what happened."

"You don't know that, do you?"

"No. But, we usually do."

"You mean, *you* usually do. I've—haven't I read about you, Inspector? In the newspapers."

"Possibly," Heimrich said. He stood up. He said, "I won't bother you any more just now, Lady Grimes. Have the stewardess bring you something. Tea or something."

"Or," she said, "a stiff whisky and soda. So I can—pull myself together."

"You're staying together very well," Heimrich told her. "You're doing fine. Amazingly fine."

She shook her head. She said, "Dreadfully. I'm—I'm breaking apart inside. You know that. You've seen that, haven't you?"

"You're in shock," he said. "There—probably there ought to be somebody with you, Lady Grimes."

"The stewardess will stay. She's—she's a very helpful person. She'll get me a good stiff drink."

Heimrich said, "Fine," and started down the passageway toward the door. He turned and came back.

"Last night," he said. "You and Sir Ronald were a little late at the comandante's cocktail party. He said something about a telephone call that had held you up. Can you tell me anything about that, Lady Grimes?"

She shook her head.

"To somebody on the ship? Or ship-to-shore?"

She shook her head again. But then she said, "He went up to the wireless room. It's on the sun deck. I went up with him. There's a little waiting room. Then we came down to the captain's party. But I don't know whom he called."

It probably didn't have anything to do with anything, he told her.

He went forward to the *veranda belvedere*. Susan was waiting on one of the little sofas. There were drinks on the table in front of her, but neither drink had been touched. When he lifted his, the glass was cold to his fingers. She raised her eyebrows. He shrugged his shoulders. Then he shook his head.

There were a good many people in the lounge. The four businessmen—the refugees from a convention—were smoking cigars and drinking apéritifs and talking loudly in French. They had, Heimrich thought, had time for several apéritifs. Major Ian Whitney was at a table alone, with a tall glass in front of him. Then Mrs. Raymond Powers came into the room. She looks, Susan thought, as if she's just been to the hairdresser. I'll try to set an appointment this afternoon. It won't be the way it was yesterday. We won't sit on the deck together and go down to our cabin and have naps together. The holiday is broken. No, not broken. The holiday is dented.

Mrs. Powers hesitated just inside the lounge and looked around it. Still, Susan thought. she's looking for her party. But then Major Whitney stood up at his table and saluted across the room, and Lucinda Powers went to his table, moving with graceful assurance on the slightly uneasy deck. Whitney pulled a chair out for her and beckoned to Mario. Lucinda Powers and the major smiled at each other.

But I had a feeling, Susan thought, that they didn't like each other—that, at the captain's party, she didn't really like any of us. I make up stories about people, and the stories fall apart. They smile and talk as if they don't know anything has happened. She turned to Merton, who had closed his eyes. But he felt her look and opened them. She said, "You saw Lady Grimes?"

"Yes. She's—it's being very hard on her. And will get harder before it gets easier. She loved him. ı think. Perhaps very much."

"It is—past tense?"

"I'm afraid so."

"And—it's been pushed onto you? But that is a foolish

85

thing to say, isn't it? 'Pushed,' I mean."

"It's my trade," Heimrich said. "And Hunt was a cop, dear. You don't want people killing cops, do you?"

"I don't want anybody killing anybody," Susan said. "And, yes, I know you have to find out about it. It's a need built into you. Even on holiday."

"I'm sorry," Heimrich said.

She smiled at him. She said, "Oh, I wouldn't have you any other way. I'll try to get an appointment to have my hair done after lunch. And if he's busy—I think there's only one—I'll sit on the deck. Or write letters. Or read a book. I'll be all right. And I won't go near the ship's railings. Mrs. Powers seems to have found her party."

"I noticed."

"Do they know about Sir Ronald? About poor Mr. Hunt?"

"I don't know, Susan. I asked Lady Grimes not to talk about it. Not yet, anyway. Oh, it will spread through the ship, naturally. Is spreading now, probably. The Grimeses have been coming here for a drink before lunch. Mario will notice when they don't come. Their waiter will notice at lunch. Their stewardess already knows. Guido found Hunt's body. It won't be in the ship's newspaper tomorrow. It won't be announced on the public-address system. It'll get around."

Emily Farrell and a woman in a pink suit came into the lounge together. "The fourth at bridge," Susan said. "She does like pink, doesn't she?"

Mario took Miss Farrell and last night's fourth at bridge to a sofa across the dance floor, and they sat facing the Heimrichs. Miss Farrell looked across at them and stood up and seemed about to cross the floor. But she merely shook her head, sadly, and sat down again.

"It's getting around," Susan said.

The chimes sounded. They finished their drinks and went down to lunch.

When they came out of the dining salon after lunch, an erect young officer, the same officer who had acted as messenger before, came up to them. He said, "Signor Inspector."

"I'll go see about an appointment," Susan said, and went toward an elevator.

Heimrich watched her as she walked across the foyer. She's got her sea legs, he thought. She's really fine, now. Damn murder to hell. He turned back to the young officer.

"The comandante's compliments," the officer said. He spoke very precisely, as a man does who has learned very well a language not his own. "He would appreciate it if you would come to his quarters, Inspector. At your convenience."

Which might mean, Heimrich thought, that di Scarlotti's security force had found Sir Ronald Grimes. Or that somebody had come forward to confess strangling Detective Inspector Hunt. Which would, of course, mean neither of those things. Di Scarlotti wanted to be kept abreast. Which would be easy enough because Heimrich was not going anywhere.

"If the signor inspector wishes—"

"I know my way," Heimrich said, and went up to the lido deck and forward through a narrow passageway to a door he was getting to know. A steward opened to his knocking. Comandante di Scarlotti got up from the table and put his coffee cup in its saucer. He said, "Coffee for the inspector," and the steward said, "Sir," and went into the other room. Heimrich sat down and accepted a cigarette and, when it came, coffee. He said, "You haven't found Sir Ronald, I take it?"

"No, Inspector," di Scarlotti said. "I regret. We have found nothing. It is—it has become almost certain he is not in the ship. You have seen Lady Grimes?"

"What she told you," Heimrich said. "Or the staff captain. Or whoever talked to her earlier. Nothing beyond that. Oh, that Sir Ronald has a son. By a previous marriage. Who is now, she's afraid, and I'm afraid, the ninth baronet. She is very much broken up, naturally. She does not know to whom her husband made a telephone call last evening."

Di Scarlotti said, "A telephone call, Inspector?"

"When he came here last evening," Heimrich said. "To your

party. He was sorry he was late. A telephone call had delayed him."

"I did not remember," di Scarlotti said. "From someone aboard *Italia*? In his cabin?"

"They went up to the wireless room, Lady Grimes says. She waited while he made a call. Or, conceivably, received one. There will be a record, Captain?"

"Most certainly."

"Probably has nothing to do with his disappearing," Heimrich said. "May have been calling anybody. His broker. His estate manager in England to ask how the roses are coming along. The British Embassy in Washington. We'll ask. And I suppose the Embassy should be notified."

"I will have a message sent. When we are certain. There is still a chance—" He broke off and shook his head and lighted a cigarette. "There is no chance," he said. "Sir Ronald went overboard. The head office—the office will be most disturbed, Inspector. A distinguished man trusts himself to my ship. He disappears. A police official is killed. It is most disturbing, Inspector. And it is my responsibility, of course."

"Not very directly," Heimrich said. "You can't be—"

He stopped because Comandante di Scarlotti was shaking his head and shaking it sadly.

"You do not understand," di Scarlotti said. "Whatever happens aboard *Italia*, or to *Italia*, is my responsibility, inspector. Things are so in my service. Years ago, Inspector, one of your naval vessels went aground in—I think it was in Chesapeake Bay. The captain of the ship did not have the con, of course. He had not plotted the course. His navigator had done that. But the captain was relieved of command, Inspector. And, he did not make admiral. It is so at sea, Inspector. Now, while we are drinking coffee, if *Italia*—oh, hits something, goes aground somewhere—it will be my responsibility.Although she is in most capable hands."

"And," Heimrich said, "in mid-Atlantic somewhere. With nothing to hit. With nothing to run into."

"An example only," di Scarlotti said. "When we go into harbor I shall be on the bridge. Particularly when we go into the harbor at Málaga. I do not like the harbor at Málaga."

Heimrich waited for some seconds. He drank more coffee. He accepted another cigarette. He said, "Your security people, Captain? They've come up with anything?"

"They have not found Sir Ronald. He was, as you told me, in the observation lounge about ten-thirty last night. Inspector Hunt was with him. The steward has verified this."

Heimrich said, "Did the steward say how long—?"

Comandante di Scarlotti said, "Sì." He said, "Sir Ronald and the inspector had one drink each. They were in the lounge for only about fifteen minutes. They went out together. We have not been able to discover that anybody saw either of them after that. Not on the decks. Not in passageways. Not in the other public rooms. Of course, at that hour—"

At that hour, except in the public rooms, the staff was reduced. Passengers who were not in the ballroom, were not in any of the several cocktail lounges or in the card room or walking around the decks, had gone to their cabins. The room stewards and stewardesses had, for the most part, gone off duty. Antonio and Rachele, who served Cabins Sixteen and Eighteen, among other cabins, had gone off duty. Guido and Angela, who served Hunt's cabin as well as that of the Heimrichs, had gone off duty. Night stewards were on duty on all the decks, but they had each many cabins to serve, if service was needed.

"The passengers are cared for, Inspector. But most of them sleep. Or, of course—most of them sleep."

None of the attendants on duty had seen either Grimes or Hunt after they left the *veranda belvedere*. They had not been seen, singly or together, in any of the rooms where they might have gone for a final drink. No drinks had been charged to either of their cabins after the one drink apiece in the *veranda belvedere*. They had not been seen going into their cabins. They had not been seen on the promenade decks—on either

89

the glass-enclosed promenade deck proper or on the boat deck above it.

"The Grimeses' suite is on the boat deck," Heimrich said. "And if he went overboard, it was most likely from that deck."

"Yes. But he was not seen."

Nor had Detective Inspector Albert Hunt been seen going into his cabin on the upper deck.

"Your doctor," Heimrich said. "Give you a guess as to when Hunt was killed?"

"He cannot be certain."

"None of them ever can," Heimrich told him. "A guess? They can always guess within—oh, within a few hours."

"Between eleven and, possibly, two in the morning, the doctor thinks. He thinks probably nearer midnight. If he had been called earlier, he could be more exact."

"About all we ever get," Heimrich said.

"We do not advance," di Scarlotti said. He shook his head. "I cannot see that we advance. You and Mrs. Heimrich. You debark at Málaga? We dock at Málaga Monday morning. Quite early Monday morning. And now it is Thursday. Thursday afternoon." He shook his head again. "We stop at Lisbon," he said. "Then at Málaga. Neither is Italian, Inspector. At Naples I shall have to report these—occurrences—to the police. It is Wednesday we dock in Naples."

"Yes," Heimrich said. "I realize there isn't all the time in the world, Captain. So—"

He stood up. Di Scarlotti stood up.

"I'll try to trace this telephone call Sir Ronald made." Heimrich said. "Or, naturally, received. You'll notify—" He stopped. "No," he said, "I'll call the British Embassy, Comandante. With your approval, of course. And I'll talk to people. And you—your men will continue to search the ship?"

"It is useless," di Scarlotti said. "But we will continue to search the ship."

₩ 7

The wireless room was on the sun deck, just aft
the bridge. From the lido deck and the captain's quarters,
Heimrich climbed a flight of stairs and pushed a door open. A
placard on the door said "Stazione Radiotelefonica Radio Tele-
grafica." Heimrich went up to a desk on one side of a waiting
room, and a man in uniform showed up behind it. He said,
"Signor?"

"Heimrich. Has the captain been in touch with you?"

"Inspector. Yes, the comandante has given his instructions,
signor. You wish to make calls? Is it not that, Signor Inspector?"

"Yesterday evening," Heimrich said. "A little before seven.
Sir Ronald Grimes made a telephone call. Ship to shore, probably. Conceivably to somebody aboard ship. But he made it
from here."

"Yes, Inspector. It was a call to London. It was—one moment, signor."

He went back into a room in which there were several men
and a great deal of equipment. He returned. "Five minutes,"

91

he said. "A little more than five minutes. It was charged to his cabin."

"You have the number he called?"

The wireless operator had the number. "Put a call through for me to that number," Heimrich told him. "And, charge it to the ship. Or to Comandante di Scarlotti."

"I have been instructed," the wireless operator said. "If the inspector will go to the first booth?"

There were two telephone booths in the waiting room, and both had numbers on their doors.

"It may be a few minutes," the operator said. "I will ring in the booth when we are through."

Heimrich opened the door of Booth One and sat on a sofa outside it. He sat for a little more than half a cigarette and the bell rang in the booth. The operator said, "We are through, signor," and a woman spoke. She had a brisk voice. But she used it only to repeat the telephone number the ship's operator had given Heimrich.

"I'm calling from a ship in mid-Atlantic," Heimrich said. "I'm trying to get some information."

"Continental Forwarding, Limited," the woman—a young woman from her voice—said. "Can I help you?"

Heimrich said he hoped so. He said that, at about seven the evening before, a call had been put through from the S.S. *Italia* to that number by Sir Ronald Grimes. He wanted to know about the call. He did not say why he wanted to know.

"From mid-Atlantic?" the girl said. "At about seven? Your time, sir?"

Heimrich resisted the temptation to say, "Naturally." Perhaps even, "Naturally, *miss*." He said, "The ship's time. Yes."

"It would have been later here," the girl said. "Hours later, I should think. No call could have been put through to this number. The office closes at five."

"A call was put through," Heimrich said. "By Sir Ronald Grimes. A call of about five minutes."

"The office was closed, sir. No call would have been answered. I fear you've made a mistake, sir."

"You're on the switchboard, I take it?"

"I am in the office of the managing director. Of the London branch. Our main offices are in Liverpool."

"And everybody had left this branch office of—what is the firm again?"

"Continental Forwarding, Limited. Yes, we closed at five. We close every afternoon at five."

"And all go home? Including the managing director?"

"Certainly."

"But the telephone is plugged through to somewhere?"

"Pardon?"

"When you leave," Heimrich said, keeping his voice patient. "you press a button or something. So that if there is a call it will ring on another phone? Perhaps in the main office in Liverpool?"

"No."

"May I speak to the managing director?"

"I am sorry. Mr. Parsons has gone for the day."

"His assistant? Anybody Sir Ronald might have spoken to? Or who might know who he spoke to?"

"Everybody has gone home. But, you do not seem to understand. No call put through to this number at the time you say would have been answered."

"A call was put through," Heimrich said. "It was answered. For about five minutes it was answered. Does the name Sir Ronald Grimes mean anything to you?"

"I'm afraid I have never heard of the gentleman, sir. Sir Ronald what, sir?"

Heimrich gave her the name again, but he thought he wasted time. He thought she knew the name. Voices can be revealing.

"This Mr. Parsons," he said. "The managing director. May I leave a message for him?"

93

"Certainly, sir. One moment, sir."

He waited the moment. The girl said, "Yes?"

"Ask him to call Inspector Heimrich—" he spelled Heimrich —"on the steamship *Italia* in the morning. Tell him it's important."

"Inspector?"

"Police inspector. Will you see he gets the message?"

"I will leave it for him. A police inspector?"

"Yes."

"I will leave the message on his desk."

"Good," Heimrich said. "And when he comes in tomorrow, remember to ask him whether he found it. Right?"

"Certainly, Inspector."

Something fishy there, Heimrich thought as he went back to the counter. He did not believe Sir Ronald had talked for five minutes to a dead telephone. He did not particularly believe in Continental Forwarding, Limited. There was nothing to pin anything on, but Merton Heimrich had a feeling that Continental Forwarding, Limited, was a front for something else. He also thought that, for the moment. it presented a blank wall with no chinks in it. A chink might be—

"Get me the British Embassy in—" Heimrich said to the wireless operator and stopped and said, "No. Get me—" and gave a number which was a string of digits, beginning with 914. "It's in New York," he said. "Westchester County."

"I will ring in Booth One when we are through to this number, signor."

Heimrich started back to the sofa and turned. "This one," he said, "charge to me. Cabin Eighty-two."

The wireless man said, "As you wish, signor." and Heimrich went to the sofa and waited for the bell. You couldn't charge a ship's captain for so ridiculous a stab in the dark. Even Charles Forniss didn't know somebody everywhere. Most places, but not everywhere.

It took a few minutes to get Lieutenant Charles Forniss,

New York State Police, on the telephone in the Hawthorne Barracks. When Forniss came on, he said, "For God's sake, M.L. You're supposed to be in Spain."

"Only headed that way," Heimrich said. "Who do you know in the British Embassy in Washington, Charley?"

"Who do I know—*where?*"

Heimrich did not repeat what he had said. It was not necessary to repeat things to Charles Forniss.

"Nobody I can think of," Forniss said. "Unless—wait."

Heimrich waited.

"Long time ago," Forniss said. "After Korea. When I was in the Corps."

To Forniss there is only one "Corps." The United States Marine Corps, of which he remains a captain, inactive duty.

"It was a long time ago," Forniss said again. "Probably he's somewhere else by now. They move them around, way I understand it. Career man, he was, I gathered. Something hush-hush, way it seemed. Young fella. British as hell. But all right when you got used to the way he talked."

"Yes," Heimrich said. "His name, Charley?"

"Mason," Forniss said. "Robert Mason."

"Did you know him well? Think he'll remember you?"

"Pretty well. We—bumped into each other now and then. I—well, I was on the hush-hush side myself in those days. Probably won't remember me. But he probably isn't there any more. You mixed up in something, M.L.?"

"A disappearance," Heimrich said. "A murder."

"You," Forniss said, "are supposed to be on leave. You're supposed to be taking care of your lady."

There was a measure of disapproval in Charles Forniss's voice. Forniss seldom disapproves of the man with whom he has worked for many years. There was also concern in his voice.

"The lady's fine," Heimrich said. "She's getting her hair done. In Spain we're going to sit in the sun and look at the Mediterranean. Robert Mason?"

95

"A long time ago," Forniss said. "Probably been somewhere else for years. May be dead, for all I know."

"Anybody may be dead," Heimrich said. "Take care of yourself, Charley."

"Yep," Charles Forniss said. "And you. And of Mrs. Heimrich. You paying for this call, M.L.?"

"Yes."

"Good-by," Forniss said. "Drop me a postcard."

Forniss was curious. He was not going to be curious when it was costing a friend money. Heimrich was smiling when he went back to the wireless man, waiting at the counter.

"The British Embassy in Washington," he said. "This is charged to the ship."

The wireless man said, "Signor." He said, "I will ring the booth when we are through."

It was longer, this time. This time it was a cigarette long and the contemplation of another. The bell rang. "We are through, signor," and, at almost the same time, a woman's voice. She said, "Embassy." Heimrich had expected something more formal—something like "Her Britannic Majesty's Washington Embassy" with a vocal courtesy thrown in.

"Mr. Robert Mason, please," Heimrich said. "Tell him I'm calling on behalf of Captain Charles Forniss."

"Sir Robert," the crisp voice corrected. "Sir Robert Mason. He is likely to be occupied. On behalf of whom?"

Heimrich repeated Forniss's name.

"I will ascertain," the voice told him, which he thought a bit more like it. He waited.

"Sir Robert Mason's office," another voice said. It was a different voice, but the intonation was the same.

Heimrich wanted to speak to Sir Robert. Captain Charles Forniss had suggested he speak to Sir Robert. The voice said, "Forniss? Will you spell—yes, Sir Robert?"

A man said, "Something happened to Charley Forniss?"

"No." Heimrich said. "You do remember him, Sir Robert?"

"Obviously. What's Charley up to now? And who are you, by the way?"

"Charley's up to being a lieutenant, New York State Police. And I'm in the same outfit. Inspector M. L. Heimrich, and—"

"Heard of you, haven't I?"

"I don't know. Possibly."

"Calling as a policeman, I gather. From where, Inspector?"

"From the liner *Italia*. Mid-Atlantic."

"Oh," Mason said. "Thought you sounded a bit fuzzy, y'know. Static." There was a pause of seconds. Then Mason said, "You said *Italia*, Inspector?"

"Yes."

"Think that's the ship Ronny took," Mason said. "On his way home to grow roses. Or, as he always says, 'cabbages.' Sir Ronald Grimes, Inspector. Happen to have run into him?"

"Yes. We've met. Actually, I'm calling about him, Sir Robert."

"Good man, Ronny. Silly rule retires a man like Ronny with years ahead."

"That's just it." Heimrich said. "I'm afraid he hadn't years ahead. He seems to have disappeared from the ship."

There was a longer pause this time. Then Mason said, "What d'you mean disappeared?"

"Just that. Last night he was having a drink in one of the lounges. Today he's—well, he's not anywhere we can find. And the ship has been searched."

"Not Ronny. Steady old horse. Must be around somewhere."

"He isn't," Heimrich said, and asked the question: "Know anybody who'd want him not to be? Anybody connected with what he was doing at the Embassy before he was retired?"

"What you're getting at," Mason said, "Somebody pushed him off the ship. That what you're getting at?"

97

"It's a possibility we're looking into," Heimrich said.

"And who are we? How do you come into it, Inspector? Not New York State, *Italia* isn't. Italian registry."

"The ship's captain asked me to lend a hand."

"You say Charley Forniss gave you my name? Eh?"

"Yes. It was Mr. Mason when he knew you."

Mason said, "Oh, that. Sort of thing can happen to anyone. This Forniss you say's a policeman. What does he look like?"

"A big man," Heimrich said, and went on to describe Charles Forniss, former Marine Corps captain, who had—Heimrich now remembered—worked for a time with Naval Intelligence before he was deactivated.

"Sounds like him. Anything special about him, Inspector?"

"If you *are* a police inspector," where the words left out of that.

"The top of his left ear is clipped off a bit," Heimrich said. "Sniper bullet. In Korea. Not especially obvious. The scar, I mean."

"All right." Mason said. "I guess it's the same Charles Forniss."

"And," Heimrich said, "I may just have met him casually somewhere. May not be a man named Heimrich at all. May be trying to put something over on you. On your service, for all you know. Suppose I hang up. Suppose you have your operator call the *Italia*. Ask for Inspector M. L. Heimrich, New York State Police. Make sure you get the right ship. Not—oh, some Russian trawler offshore. Because—"

"All right," Mason said. "You can come off it now, Inspector. No use running up Embassy expenses with a trunk call, eh? No. I don't know anybody connected with our service who'd want to harm Ronald Grimes. Or connected with anything. I don't know anybody who didn't like him. Respect him, come to that. Fine old family. Army people, mostly. Ronny was an exception to the Grimes rule. And—a good man. A damn good man. The Foreign Office was half-witted to let him go. Not that it isn't from time to time, y'know. And don't quote me."

"Every big establishment is half-witted from time to time," Heimrich said. "Sir Ronald was commercial attaché at the Embassy?"

"What it came to. Smoothing pathways for our exporters. Balance-of-trade sort of thing, y'know. Good at it, Ronny was."

"And American firms which wanted to export to Britain?"

"Came into it, I suppose. Not my line of country, y'know. Not likely anything in his work would lead to what's happened. What you're afraid's happened. You and the ship's captain. What's his name, by the way?"

A diplomat needs to learn caution. Now and then. Heimrich thought, caution surfaces.

"Comandante Antonio di Scarlotti. Would you like to speak to him, Sir Robert? To—reassure yourself?"

"No," Mason said. "Anyway, my Italian's a bit rusty."

"His English isn't in the least. So if—"

"All right," Mason said. "Sorry, Inspector. Sort of thing that's a bit rubbed into us, y'know."

"Do you know whether Sir Ronald had much contact with a man named Raymond Powers? Industrialist of some sort. He—"

"I know who he is," Mason said. "Was, rather. Popped off a while back. Captain-of-industry type." The words echoed faintly in Heimrich's mind. "'Powers Industries, Incorporated,' I think it was. Manufactures heavy machinery, way I understand it. Machine tools. Probably has a hand in a dozen other things. Baby powder, for all I know. Diversification, they call it here."

"I know," Heimrich said. "I live there, Sir Robert. Would Powers and Sir Ronald have had contact? Consulted about— oh, exports and imports. That sort of thing?"

"Might have." Mason said. "Come to think of it, I think they did. Yes. Ran into Ronny and Ellen someplace. Restau-

99

rant, probably. They were with the Powerses, the Grimeses were. Listen, this is tough on Ellen. Lady Grimes."

"Very," Heimrich said. "You and Lady—I take it there is a Lady Mason?"

"Yes, Inspector. There is indeed. Were we introduced to Mr. and Mrs. Powers? Yes. Didn't linger. We were going on somewhere."

There was a momentary pause.

"Why do you ask about Mr. and Mrs. Powers, Inspector? Do they come into it?"

"Not that I know of," Heimrich said. "Only thing is, Mrs. Powers is on board. I gather she knew Sir Ronald in Washington. Just—call it confirming. The way you confirmed Charley Forniss."

"Black hair with a white streak in it. Very artful white streak. Good figure. In her forties, at a guess."

"Yes," Heimrich said.

"Confirmed," Sir Robert said. "Same woman Betty and I were introduced to. Hard thing to forget, that white streak."

"When did Mr. Powers die, do you happen to know?"

"Good Lord, Inspector. I didn't know the fella. Oh—year ago, more or less. Good bit about in the press. Self-made and all that sort of thing. Sort of chap we make Lord somebody, apparently. Starts in a foundry. Ends up with millions. Labor peer, probably."

"Anything odd about his death, that you remember?"

"Heart attack, I think. Wait a minute. He was walking along the street. Couple of blocks from the Embassy, actually. From half a dozen embassies, come to that. Tend to cluster, y'know. Walking along and just dropped dead. Happens, y'know. Happened to your Adlai Stevenson pretty much the same way. Good man, Stevenson. Ran into him a few times. He—wait a minute."

Heimrich waited, but not for a minute.

"Getting back to Powers," Sir Robert said. "Remember now.

According to the newspapers, Powers had been here—at the Embassy—just before he popped off. Conferring with an Embassy official. That's the way it was put."

"Sir Ronald Grimes?"

"Could have been, I expect. Could be checked back on, probably. Take a bit of doing, I'd think. Not get you anywhere, would it? What I mean is, Ronny didn't feed him poison in a drink, y'know. The old ticker just stopped. Post mortem and all that sort of thing."

"No need to check on that," Heimrich said. "Not that I can see, anyway. Sir Robert. there's another man who seems to be connected with your Embassy aboard the Italia. Not with Sir Ronald, but knew him. A man named Whitney. Major Ian Whitney."

"A military attaché," Mason said. "We've got them by dozens, y'know. All services. Keeping an eye on what you Yanks are up to. Yes, I know Whitney. Slightly. Only been here a couple of years. Got thrown out of one of the Iron Curtain countries, I think. Doesn't mean anything. We throw theirs out; they throw ours out. We catch theirs and trade them for ones they've caught of ours. Matter of routine, it's pretty much got to be."

"Charges against the major? In wherever he was stationed?"

"Poland, as I recall it. No. Just *persona non grata*. So we picked one of theirs. Comparable rank and that sort of thing, and non-grataed him. All in the family, in a way of speaking. Sort of thing that's been going on for hundreds of years, actually. Come down to it, Inspector, foreign offices are foreign offices and always have been. If you mean, was Whitney spying, I'd doubt it. Not the type, I'd think. Proper career officer, y'know. Not Sandhurst, I think. Oxford. Could be Cambridge, of course. Not a cloak-and-dagger sort, Whitney isn't. Be retired a colonel, shouldn't wonder. Live in the midlands and grow vegetable marrows and be a member of the hunt and—"

Very abruptly, Robert Mason stopped speaking. He was silent for some seconds, and when he spoke again, his voice was different. It had been light and casual as he talked of Powers and Major Ian Whitney. Now it was slow. There was almost a catch in it.

"Damn it all," Robert Mason said, "Ronny was a friend of mine. Going back to this big place of his in the country and grow roses. Or, he always said, cabbages. What I mean is, damn it all. You're sure he's not on the ship somewhere?"

"Pretty sure," Heimrich said.

"Good chap," Sir Robert said. "Damn good chap."

"Do you know, Sir Robert, why he decided to go back home by ship? And by a rather roundabout way, come to that?"

"No. Oh, for the rest, I'd think. And—well, there wasn't any hurry, y'know. He was through with hurrying. And—well, it's pretty wet and cold in England this time of year. Spring here in Washington, you know. Been stationed here a long time, Ronny had. Taking the climate change in easy stages, shouldn't wonder. Stay a while in Italy, perhaps. Wait for spring to move north, y'know."

"Probably the reason," Heimrich said. "Does this mean anything to you, Sir Robert?"

He quoted digits; the digits of the telephone number of Continental Forwarding, Limited.

And there was, for rather a long time, no answer. When Robert Mason answered, it was with one word, and the word spoken in a different tone. Sir Robert's voice was hard, demanding. But all he said was, "Why?"

"Grimes called it from the ship yesterday evening. He talked, according to the record, for five minutes or more. I called it myself today. I was told that it was something called 'Continental Forwarding, Limited.' And that Sir Ronald could not have called that number at the time he did because the office was closed and he would not have been answered. The number mean anything to you, Sir Robert? Or 'Continental Forwarding'?"

"Not a thing."

The voice remained hard. Now it was final.

"Does the name Detective Inspector Albert Hunt mean anything to you? British, he was."

"Not a thing," Robert Mason said again. "Supposed to?"

"I don't kncw," Heimrich said. "He was on the ship too, Sir Robert. And sometime last night he was strangled in his cabin."

"The hell—"

And then abrupt silence.

"Afraid I never heard of this man Hunt," Sir Robert Mason said. "Policeman, I gather?"

"Yes. Lady Grimes thinks he was what you call Special Branch. Still doesn't ring a bell, Sir Robert?"

"Not a bell. Isn't a call of this length running you into money, Inspector?"

"Not me," Heimrich said. "The Italian Line. But good of you to give me so much of your time, Sir Robert."

"Nothing of it," Robert Mason said in his office in Washington. "Remember me to Charley Forniss, will you?"

And then Mason hung up.

♨ 8

Heimrich went out of the telephone booth and started to go out of the wireless room. But, instead, he sat down on one of the waiting-room sofas and closed his eyes. At his desk, the wireless man looked at him, but the wireless man was not looked at.

Sir Robert Mason, who had been cordial, who had even been chatty, had suddenly frozen. A London telephone number and a name had frozen him. Mason had never heard of the number, and that Heimrich found he did not believe. Mason had never heard of Detective Inspector Albert Hunt. That might well be true. Hunt had been, Heimrich thought, a man who might well remain as unheard-of as he had been so nearly invisible. It was entirely possible that he had preferred to be unknown and markedly inconspicuous. The preference might well have been professional.

What was the name of that chief inspector at Scotland Yard I met three or four years ago? When I flew to London to have a look at a man and, if he turned out to be the right man, to bring him back? He did turn out to be the right man, and I did bring him back and—*Walling*. That was the chief inspector's name. Cooperative sort of person, as chief inspectors go. Won't remember me, of course. A State Police captain flying over to pick up a man wanted on a murder charge. We did have a couple in a pub. I had to explain to the barmaid how to make a martini. She didn't learn very rapidly or, as it turned out, very well. Walling helped me explain. But he won't remember. And, whether he remembers or not, he probably won't talk. He'll probably freeze up, the way Mason froze up. Still—

He got up and went over to the desk, and the wireless man said, "Signor?"

"The metropolitan police in London," Heimrich said. "See if you can get them for me."

"That would be Scotland Yard, Inspector?"

It would be Scotland Yard. It also would be charged to the ship. "Signor. If you will—"

Heimrich went back and waited on the sofa near Booth One.

Scotland Yard had been a major disappointment those three or four years ago. He knew that New Scotland Yard had moved out of its ancient quarters on the Thames, which he had read about but never seen—in which police officers sat in offices and looked out over the river and were brought tea while they solved crimes. But he had not been prepared for the newer Scotland Yard—for a starkly rectangular building which might have been moved over to London from Park Avenue; which was fully air-conditioned and brightly lighted and completely without character. He had been offered a tour of the "black museum," which had been moved over from the old building, but he had declined. He knew what instruments people used to kill other people and what people looked like after they had been killed. And he knew enough of other instruments used for other purposes on human bodies.

But he had not been a tourist. He had been a policeman on a job and—

The bell rang in the booth, and Heimrich went into it and

105

was told that they were through, signor, and heard, "Metropolitan police, Detective Constable Smothers." At least it sounded like "Smothers"—"Smothers" with static in it. Heimrich said he would like to speak to Chief Inspector Walling and, being asked, said who was calling. He spelled his name. He waited the one moment stipulated, and a man said, "Chief Inspector Walling's office."

Heimrich would like to speak to the chief inspector. He said who would like to speak to the chief inspector and spelled his name again. He waited the stipulated moment. A gruff voice said, "Walling here."

"You won't remember me," Heimrich said. "Three-four years ago. You people caught a man for the State of New York, and I—"

"I remember you," Walling said. "Had a hell of a time getting a cocktail the way you wanted it. Had to give you a hand up myself, as I remember it. You were a captain then. Gone up a notch, apparently. What can I do for you, Heimrich?"

"I'm calling from an Italian liner in mid-Atlantic," Heimrich said. "About one of your men. Man named Hunt. Detective Inspector Albert Hunt."

"What about him?"

"He's been killed. Strangled in his cabin on the S.S. *Italia*. And another man has disappeared from the ship."

Walling said, "Hmmm," with a rising inflection.

"Hunt's your man," Heimrich said. "I thought your department would want to know what's happened to him. And the man missing is Sir Ronald Grimes."

"Heard of Grimes. He'll be a loss to his service. You're saying he *is* a loss, I take it?"

"He appears to be."

"Signal to the Foreign Office about him, I'd think."

"The *Italia*'s captain will send a message," Heimrich said. "When they've finished searching the ship. About Hunt?"

"Heimrich, we've got a lot of detective inspectors. You said 'Albert Hunt'?"

"Yes."

"Don't know that I—wait a minute. Rather small man? Easy man to overlook?"

"That's the man, Chief Inspector."

"Seems to me he's not here. That is, he's Special Branch. Kind of man who would be. All very hush-hush in Special Branch, y'know."

"You've no idea what he was doing on the ship? I mean, pleasure cruise or job?"

"No. Not one of my men. I told you that, didn't I?"

"Yes. Can you put me on to somebody who might know? The captain of the ship's asked me to lend a hand."

"Just happened to be around? You, I mean?"

"Just happened to be around. On leave."

"Pity. For you, I mean. Your wife's with you? I mean, seem to remember you've got a wife."

"I have. She's with me. This does break in on things."

"Hammond's the man," Chief Inspector Walling said. "If Hunt was on a job, Hammond will know what it was. Chief Inspector Hammond. Point is, if Hunt was on a job, Hammond won't tell you what it was."

"All the same. Can you have me switched to Chief Inspector Hammond? And—oh, vouch for me? So I'm not a strange voice out of nowhere?"

"Waste of your time, probably. Very hush-hush. But it is your time, isn't it? Hold on a minute." Heimrich held. He heard jumbled voices. Then, again, he heard Walling's gruff voice. "Getting him on." Walling said. "By the way—that cocktail you had so much trouble getting. Good when you got it?"

"Not very."

"Low-proof gin, that's what it is," Walling said. "Everything worth drinking goes to the States. Here he is, Hammond."

Another voice—a sharper voice—said, "Inspector Heimrich? What's this about Hunt? Hammond here."

"Hunt's been killed," Heimrich said. "Strangled in his cabin on a ship named *Italia*. I'm trying to find out who killed him. I happen to be aboard the *Italia*."

"Police inspector, Walling says you are. Just happen to be aboard?"

You have to answer the same question a good many times. Heimrich told Chief Inspector Hammond that he had just happened to be aboard and that he had been asked by the ship's captain to help out. To this Hammond said, "Hmmm." Then he said, "State or federal?" It was Heimrich's turn to say, "Hmmm?"

"What kind of a policeman?" Hammond said. "City? State? Federal?" His sharp voice was patient—noticeably patient.

"New York State Police," Heimrich said, his own voice patient. "Bureau of Criminal Investigation. Troop K, Hawthorne Barracks. Which is in—"

"All right, man," Hammond said. "All *right*."

"About Detective Inspector Hunt," Heimrich said. "Who was strangled in his cabin. He was with the Special Branch?"

Hammond apparently gave that consideration. After a pause, he said, "He was. Yes."

"Your Special Branch," Heimrich said. "I understand it's interested in—call it international matters. As they concern your national security."

Hammond said, "Do you, Inspector?"

Heimrich waited.

"We're concerned with various matters," Hammond said.

It was evident from his tone that the various matters were not a concern of a New York State policeman, inspector or not.

"Hunt," Heimrich said. "He was taking a sea voyage. For his health? Or on business?"

"Far's I know," Hammond said, "Bert Hunt was healthy. Not young. Not a big man. Just over our minimum, come to that. But healthy enough."

"On leave?"

"Have to consult the records on that one."

The tone did not imply that consultation of the records was on the immediate agenda.

"I met Hunt only once," Heimrich said. "Sir Ronald Grimes introduced him. Hunt said something about a man in New York he—I think he said, 'we wanted a word with.' So I assumed he was on a job."

"Did you?"

"Chief Inspector, Hunt was one of your men. He's been killed. I think while on duty. Don't you give a damn? Our force, we don't like our men being killed."

"Yes," Hammond said, "we give a damn, Heimrich."

"Sir Ronald Gimes," Heimrich said. "In your diplomatic service. Knew Hunt, apparently. Sir Ronald's disappeared."

"So Walling told me before you came on," Hammond said. "Loss to his service." Hammond paused. "To the country, come to that," he added. There was a slight modification in the sharpness of his voice.

"Sir Ronald's disappearance from the ship," Heimrich said. "Probably went overboard. Hunt's murder. There's obviously a connection, wouldn't you say?"

"You're there," Hammond said. "I'm not."

"Sir Ronald and Hunt were having drinks together," Heimrich said. "Shortly before Hunt was killed. Before Sir Ronald disappeared."

"Interesting."

"But not interesting enough to persuade you to tell me what Hunt was doing on the ship?"

"Sorry. No."

"But you know."

Hammond did not answer that.

"You're very hush-hush, aren't you? As Walling said you'd be."

"You can call it that, Heimrich. Some things are—classified."

"You're not being helpful, are you? For all Hunt's having been one of your men."

"Put that way, no, I suppose I'm not. Sorry and all that."

There was another slight change in Chief Inspector Hammond's voice—enough of a change to make Heimrich think that perhaps Hammond was sorry.

Heimrich said, "Nice to know. Good-by, Chief Inspector."

There was a stone wall around it, Heimrich thought in the waiting room of the *Italia*'s wireless station. It was a wall of official stones. And I, he thought, am not really under any obligation to pull those stones apart. I'm a policeman, but one far out his jurisdiction and one on leave. This is eating into our holiday, and Susan needs her holiday. I can chuck it. I can tell Comandante di Scarlotti that it's none of my business; tell him it's all up to his security force. (Which hasn't sense enough to take pictures of the body of a murdered man before they move the body.)

Sir Ronald was a pleasant man, on his way home to grow roses. With, he thought, quite a few years ahead to grow them in. (Or cabbages, of course.) But he was a man, and his wife a woman, I'd met only casually; would never have met again after we leave the ship at Málaga. I have no personal concern; no official concern. Sir Ronald's death is a murder—if it is a murder—I can let somebody get away with. There's no doubt that Hunt was murdered, but—

I didn't exchange half a dozen words with Detective Inspector Albert Hunt. Grimes was nothing to me—a pleasant man met on shipboard. Hunt was even less. Only—all right, Hunt was a cop. A lot of cops get killed. Getting killed is a risk a cop contracts for. He was a cop somebody had built a stone wall around, and nobody is going to thank me for pulling at the stones.

"Something there is that doesn't love a wall." That was Frost. Susan likes to read us Frost. There's something in me that doesn't love a wall. Susan said something like that. She wants her holiday. She doesn't want me hacking away at a wall, with singularly bare hands to do the hacking. But she

110

said something about its being the way I am and something about liking the way I am. All the same—

He realized he was standing near the door with his eyes closed. He opened them. The wireless man was looking at him. The wireless man said, "Will there be anything else, signor?"

"I guess—" Heimrich said, and stopped himself before "not."

"Do your records show any calls—ship-to-shore calls—charged to Albert Hunt? Cabin One-oh-eight, I think it is."

The wireless man could look up the records. Heimrich waited while he looked up the records. There were no ship-to-shore calls charged against Cabin 108. Was there anything more?

Heimrich said there wasn't anything more. He went down a flight of stairs and took an elevator "below" to the "upper" deck. He might as well have a look at the cabin Hunt had died in. Although it had, probably, been cleaned up. The sheets a man had writhed in while trying to stay alive would have been removed. The bed would be newly and neatly made.

On the upper deck. Heimrich walked aft on the starboard side of *Italia*. He walked past Cabin 82 and was tempted to go into it. Susan might have returned from the hairdresser; she might be in the cabin. He went on aft through the corridor and came to Cabin 108. He tried the door and found it locked. But then Guido was behind him and said, "Signor Inspector?"

"I want to get into Hunt's cabin," Heimrich said. "Have a look at it. You've been told to help me?"

Guido said, "But certainly, Signor Inspector" and unlocked the door of Cabin 108. Heimrich went into the cabin, and Guido stood outside it, looking in.

It was a small cabin, inboard of the ship. There was one bed and one place to hang clothes, and the bathroom which opened off had a glass-enclosed shower and no tub. But it was enough cabin for a man traveling alone.

It had not been made up. Sheets trailed from the bed. and the pillows were on the deck beside the bed. "We were told to

111

wait," Guido said. Heimrich said, "Good," his voice abstracted. The tangled bed in which a man had died wasn't going to tell him anything. A business suit—a neutral gray business suit—hung on a hanger in the open closet space and a tweed jacket, also gray, and slacks hung beside it. Heimrich went through pockets. He found part of a pack of Gold Flakes and a folder of matches.

"His wallet?" Heimrich said over his shoulder. "His papers. Keys. Things like that?"

"The *commissario*, signor. The purser's office. In the safe."

There was one moderate-size suitcase in the luggage racks, constructed to hold many cases.

Heimrich took the suitcase off the rack and opened it. It was empty. No, there was a paper clip in a corner. Heimrich closed the case and put it back on the rack. He said, over his shoulder, "All the luggage he had, Guido?"

"I think there was one other," Guido said. "A small, flat case. Such as he might have carried papers in, signor. I cannot be sure, but that is what I think."

"The purser's office?"

"Probably, signor."

"When you'd come in in the mornings," Heimrich said, "to bring his breakfast—how would the place look, Guido?"

"Pardon, signor?"

"Things strewn around?"

"No. His dinner things hung up, signor. His shirt hung up. His underthings folded and on the chair. On the dressing table, his billfold. Keys. Cigarettes and matches. signor."

There were drawers for shirts and handkerchiefs and socks and shorts. Heimrich opened them. Hunt had traveled light. He had traveled neatly. He had a dinner shirt and two grayish blue dress shirts and a gray sports shirt to go with sports jacket and slacks. He had socks and ten handkerchiefs and half a dozen pairs of shorts. The shirts and the shorts had labels of a London haberdasher. They had not, Heimrich thought, cost Albert Hunt very much.

112

There was a dark gray necktie, to go with the business suit. And a black tie, almost certainly the one that had been found on the deck, was in the drawer beside the gray one.

"He was dressed when you found him. I mean, in a dinner jacket?"

"Yes, signor."

"Still on the body when it was taken to the hospital?"

"Yes, signor."

There was nothing in the cabin. It was as unassuming, as negative, as Hunt himself had been.

Heimrich went down to the foyer deck and found the office of the purser. A man in uniform, with thinning black hair, said, "Certainly, Inspector. We have been instructed." He opened a safe and put a wallet on a table and a ring with two keys on it. He said, "The properties of Inspector Hunt, signor."

There was a warrant card in the billfold and a few other cards of identification. There were $215 in American banknotes and a sheaf of American Express checks. The checks added up to $500. It was a new traveler's-check folder. No checks had been used out of it. Tucked in a compartment of the wallet were two 500-lira notes. In a change compartment there were English coins and some American and several pesetas. Which did not necessarily mean that Hunt had planned to go ashore at Lisbon.

Nothing meant anything, except that Detective Inspector Albert Hunt had been Detective Inspector Albert Hunt and could have proved it.

"There was a case," Heimrich said. "An attaché case, apparently. May I see that?"

He got spread hands and shrugged shoulders and a shaken head. He got, "No such case was given us, signor. One of my assistants collected Signor Hunt's effects for safekeeping. Alonzo?"

Alonzo was a younger officer, and he said, "Signor?"

There had been no such flat case in Signor Hunt's cabin. A

113

large suitcase, which was empty. Clothing. Nothing which needed to be put in the safe.

"The steward remembers seeing such a case," Heimrich said. "Hunt spoke of working on a report. He probably carried papers in an attaché case."

"It was not there when I brought Signor Hunt's possessions from his cabin," Alonzo said. "There was no such case, Inspector. The steward could be mistaken, no?"

"I doubt if he was," Heimrich said, and went out of the purser's office and down a flight of stairs to A deck and the hospital. The doctor, who had pronounced Hunt dead and guessed at a time of his death, was busy. He was holding a stethoscope against the chest of an eight-year-old boy, who was very much alive and proving it by wriggling. A woman in her thirties and, for Heimrich's taste, somewhat overrounded, said, "How is he, Doctor?"

"He's got no fever," the doctor said. "Chest sounds fine. A slight cold, perhaps, signora. A few hours in bed, signora. Perhaps a gentle laxative."

The eight-year-old was taken out. The doctor said, "*Mothers.*" He looked up at Heimrich. He said, "You look fit enough, signor."

"Heimrich. About the man who was strangled, Doctor."

"Inspector," the doctor said. "The comandante advised me. You wish to see the body?"

Heimrich did not, particularly. He has seen many bodies. He said, "Just tell me, Doctor."

"Manual strangulation," the doctor said. "He died between eleven and probably, about two in the morning. He died quickly, Inspector. The carotid artery plexus was crushed."

"Someone with strong hands?"

The doctor shrugged.

"Probably," he said. "But someone who knew where to press—who can say? The carotid artery area is fragile, Inspector. Special strength would not have been needed."

114

"A woman might have been strong enough?"

The doctor shrugged again. "Many women are of considerable strength, signor. If the inspector wishes to view the body?"

Heimrich said, again, that he did not want to look at the body of the late Detective Inspector Hunt. He said, "That will keep." Then he added, "I suppose it will, Doctor?"

"Certainly," the doctor said. "We have most adequate facilities, Inspector. Most ample. For any emergency."

The doctor was, Heimrich thought, going back to the upper deck by elevator, a shade complacent about it. He somehow managed to imply that, if it became necessary, the bodies of all the *Italia*'s passengers could be efficiently refrigerated.

⚔ 9

The elevator was small, and Heimrich is not. But there was enough room in the elevator for one man, however large; there was no reason for Merton Heimrich to feel trapped in it. Nevertheless, he felt trapped as the elevator, with dignity and at leisure, rose from A deck to the upper deck. But it was not the elevator which trapped him. It was the ship. More precisely, it was the circumstances under which, with less than his usual confidence, he was working. The elevator stopped and opened its door, and Heimrich went out onto the *ponte superiore.*

He was cut off from the conditions, the established conditions, which made criminal investigation a reasonable occupation and gave it a chance of success. It had not occurred to anybody to photograph the body of Detective Inspector Hunt. That was a small thing; quite probably the clearest of photographs would have helped little. He had no staff; there were no detectives and no troopers to visit people and ask them questions. There was no Lieutenant Charles Forniss to do the things Forniss did so well. There was only a telephone, which

116

tended to sound somewhat muzzy, and at the distant other ends, people who set up stone walls. And he could not shut his eyes and listen to their voices as they talked nor open his eyes and watch their faces.

Continental Forwarding, Limited, was more than that, and the girl who had answered the telephone there had, of course, been lying. Robert Mason—Sir Robert Mason—in Washington knew what it was, but Sir Robert wasn't saying. Hunt had been working on something. Chief Inspector Hammond wasn't saying what.

The telephone is abrupt. A telephone receiver can be put down firmly in its cradle. The telephone inhibits patient inquiry; the slow turning over of facts and statements about facts and the looking at them from the other side—with eyes open to watch faces and closed to concentrate on the inflections of voices.

I'm alone on this, Heimrich thought. These people are the shadows of people, and I cannot dig into their backgrounds and find the substances of the people. These are shipboard acquaintances, without pasts or characters I can guess at with the knowledge to make guessing possible. It is work in a vacuum. A man named Sir Ronald Grimes has disappeared. Possibly he was pushed over the side. Possibly he climbed over the rail and let himself drop into the Atlantic Ocean. A man named Albert Hunt has been strangled, and an attaché case he had has been stolen. If Guido is right. I wonder if Grimes also had an attaché case, and whether it is in his cabin?

He had been walking aft through the port passageway of the upper deck. He was thinking about murder, and also he was thinking about Susan. This was spoiling her holiday, and she needed her holiday. He was not worried about her now—not worried as he had been worried. Still—

The hairdressing salon opened off the port passageway. She had been going to get her hair done, if she could get an appointment. He looked into the large window of the hairdresser's

117

place. A woman was sitting in a barber's chair, and a hand-some, dark young man in a green smock buttoned up at the neck was brushing her hair. Her hair was a rather startling shade of yellow. A woman was sitting under a dryer, which partly obscured her face. But it was not Susan's face. Probably Susan was in her deck chair on the promenade deck, and probably she was wondering what had become of him, as so often she had to wonder. This was a holiday; this was a time when they were to have been together. Damn it to hell. Damn the whole of it to hell, including Comandante Antonio di Scarlotti.

Heimrich crossed through the ship and went down the starboard passageway to Cabin 82. He opened the door, and Susan said, "Merton?" and he went on into the cabin.

She was standing in front of the tall mirror, and she was, thoughtfully, combing her hair. Her hair shone under the overhead light, and there seemed to be a ripple in it. It also seemed shorter than it had at lunch. But it is never long.

"I don't know that I like it," she said, and touched the ripple in her hair. "But he wanted to and I let him. But I like the cut, don't you?"

Heimrich said it was a fine cut. He said he liked the curl, if the ripple was a curl. She turned from the mirror and he looked at her carefully. She looked all right. She looked more than all right. The sparkle was back. He sat down on his bed, and she looked at him, and he answered the question she asked only with just raised eyebrows.

"No," Merton Heimrich said, "I'm not getting anywhere. I've made a few telephone calls. There's something very hush-hush about it."

"Hush-hush?"

"Restricted information," he said. "From me, anyway. Top secret, for all I know."

"Spies," Susan said. "Atomic secrets."

"I doubt if there are atomic secrets any more," Heimrich said. "Oh, there are secrets, of course. And somebody apparently did make off with an attaché case of Hunt's."

118

She raised inquiring eyebrows.

"All I know," Merton Heimrich said. "Or am likely to, probably. The report he was working on, perhaps. If he was working on a report. And perhaps extra socks and last Monday's crossword from the New York *Times*."

Susan said, "Mmmm." Then she said, "Mrs. Powers isn't hush-hush. She thinks Sir Ronald caused her husband's death. She's—she's bitter about it, Merton. She's an odd woman. She spills things out."

He waited.

"She was at the hairdresser's when I was," Susan said. "We had to wait. One of the operators was at lunch. The other one was setting somebody's hair. So we said good afternoon, and she began to talk about her husband."

"*The* Raymond Powers," Heimrich said. "The great man who worked himself to death for his country. And, I'd have guessed, for his corporation. Blames Grimes for his death? He died of a heart attack. Fell dead in Washington near—" He paused. "Near the British Embassy," he said. "Where he may have been seeing Grimes. But you can't cause a man to have a heart attack. Oh, I suppose you can. Shock him into it. But only if he's ready to have one anyway. Or, does she think it wasn't a heart attack?"

"She's not clear," Susan said, and went across the cabin and sat on her own bed, so that they faced each other across the little room. "She's—oh, she's not entirely coherent about it. And I think she may have had several drinks before lunch and they hadn't worn off. But perhaps she's always like that. It's hard to tell about people you've only just met. It was something about Sir Ronald's having blocked Powers on something very important. A business thing, she says. Something vital to the country. Either she doesn't know what, or she's not saying what. I think she doesn't know. She said, 'Ronald Grimes tormented Ray. And he knew Ray hadn't been well.' And then she said, 'It's as if he'd murdered Ray.' She said that a good many times, actually. She talked very fast, but her voice was

119

always low. Part of the time I could hardly hear her. And after a while I didn't much want to. Merton, I'm a stranger to her. And to—to go on and on."

"Probably you're right about the extra drinks," Heimrich said. "At the captain's party—what you called the V.I.P. party —she switched from sherry to vodka martinis. Extra dry vodka martinis. And she needled Sir Ronald. She was a little high, actually. And took an elevator down instead of walking down."

"I didn't pick it up about the martinis," Susan said. "Going down by elevator—yes. Not that I didn't think of that myself. But—well, Comandante di Scarlotti apparently expected us to walk down. You think today—when she was talking to me— she was high?"

She said the last with doubt in her voice. Heimrich waited.

"She seemed," Susan said, "Oh—almost hysterical. In a low-keyed sort of way. There was something in her voice. Strange in her voice. And she kept on talking about her husband and Sir Ronald—on and on. To someone she'd only met."

"Some people are like that," Heimrich said. "Find it easier to talk to strangers. Rattle on with strangers. This business about Grimes tormenting Powers? Bringing on his heart attack? That was all she rattled on about?"

It was mostly that, Susan told him. That over and over. But—

"She said, 'Calling somebody a lady doesn't have to make her a lady. You know what I mean?' I said I didn't know what she meant. I said if she was talking about Lady Grimes, I thought Lady Grimes was charming. Probably I was a little abrupt about it. I was—well, I suppose I was trying to shut her off. Because, by then, I'd pretty much had it."

"Did it shut her off?"

"No. She said, 'Oh, you do, do you?' and her voice was— well, the way it got to be at the party. Strident. Except she still didn't speak loudly, as she did part of the time at the party. I said, yes, I thought Ellen Grimes was very charming. And she said—I don't remember exactly what she said; I was just want-

120

ing it to end—but something like, 'You're not the only one who thinks that. There's that major of hers.' Something like that. And with a certain tone in her voice. An—implication."

"Whitney?"

"She just said, 'That major of hers.' I thought of Whitney, of course. It—there seemed to be an echo from somewhere."

"From the party, Susan. Mrs. Powers told Whitney he hadn't known her husband. And that she wasn't talking to him, anyway. Whitney, that is. And Whitney said something about having run into Powers now and then and added, 'Right, Ellen?' And she said something about not knowing who he'd run into, and he called her 'Lady Grimes' instead of 'Ellen' and was waspish about it. In a gentlemanly sort of way, of course."

"You listen, don't you? More than you seem to be listening."

"Acquired characteristic. Habit of the trade. Hinting that Whitney and Lady Grimes were playing around together?"

"It sounded that way. Yes. Or, I suppose, some other major. There must be a lot of majors in Washington."

"Full of them, I'd think," Heimrich said.

He closed his eyes. It was Susan's turn to wait.

"Probably Grimes's estate is entailed," he said. "Goes to his son, along with the baronetcy. But, at least a settlement on Lady Grimes. Substantial if the estate was substantial, and I suspect it was. Damn." He opened his eyes at the "Damn."

"Why?" Susan said. "I mean, why 'damn?'"

"Because we're locked up in this ship," Heimrich said. "I can't get about and ask questions. About simple little things I'd like to know. Were Major Whitney and Ellen Grimes playing around? People would have seen them if they were. Gossiped about it. People I could find or Charley Forniss could find. Cooped up. That's why the 'damn,' dear. Does Grimes leave a big estate? And does his widow get a big part of it? And does our very proper major like money? And need it? And—"

"*Merton.*" It was said in a stopping tone. He stopped.

121

"Ellen Grimes *is* charming. She's also sweet. And she was in love with her husband, and he was in love with her. I mean *in* love, darling. *In.* You could—oh, you could feel it. You felt it yourself. It's not like you to be—obtuse. Years back, when—before we were married when you—when you couldn't get it through your thick head that I was—then I used to think you were—I thought, 'Oaf.' But—"

Heimrich got up and crossed the cabin. He put his arms around his wife and pulled her up and held her close and kissed her hard. He let her sit back on the bed.

"Lady Grimes is a most charming person," he said. "She loved her husband dearly. And I'm a cop. Full of nasty suspicions."

"*You!*" Susan Heimrich said. And then she said, rather thoughtfully, "I do love you, Merton."

They looked at each other for rather a long time. Then Merton Heimrich went back across the cabin and sat down again on his own bed.

"She didn't go on with that?" he said. "Mrs. Powers, I mean. About Lady Grimes and this unidentified major?"

"No. The operator came back from lunch, and she had her hair washed. She probably has it washed every day. And then the other operator was free, and I had mine washed, and he set the wave in it and cut it. With a razor, and very well, I think. And—"

The cabin telephone rang. Susan was nearest and reached for it and said, "Yes?" into it. Then she said, "Yes, he is," and held the telephone toward Heimrich, and he took two steps across the cabin and took the telephone and said, "Heimrich."

"Whitney here. Wonder if you've got a few minutes? About Grimes, poor old chap. Because—"

"Yes," Heimrich said. "I've got a few minutes, Major. Where?"

"My cabin? Could have a spot of tea brought in, I'd think. Cabin Ten. Boat deck. Right?"

"Ten minutes," Heimrich said, and put the receiver back. He said, "Well." He closed his eyes for a moment and said, "Well," again.

"I could hear him," Susan said. "He has a carrying voice. Stiff, but carrying. You're not really fond of tea, are you?"

He smiled down at her. He said, "A policeman's lot and so forth. You?"

"A nap," Susan said. "You won't get lost, will you?"

He promised he would not get lost. He went out of Cabin 82 and up by elevator to the boat deck and along the starboard passageway to Cabin 10. He knocked on the door of Cabin 10. It was opened almost immediately.

Major Ian Whitney stood very erect; his shoulders were very square under a blue polo shirt; his mustache was crisp—a mustache of command. He was a handsome man, Heimrich thought. A good many women probably thought him an attractive man. He said, "Good man," and Heimrich followed him through a short corridor into his cabin. There was a single bed in it and a chair and a mirror and a chest of drawers. In the wall on the right as Heimrich followed the erect major into the room, there was a door. It led, Heimrich thought, into the adjacent cabin. It was closed.

"Have a pew," Whitney said, and motioned toward the chair. "Tea ought to be along. Stuffed in bags, I expect. The way you Yanks like it, what?"

"Some do," Heimrich said, and sat on the indicated chair. Whitney sat on the bed. He said, "Something stronger, Inspector? Spot of whisky?"

"Rather early," Heimrich said. "You said about—"

The door buzzer sounded. Whitney said, "Yes?" across the room, and the door to the passageway opened, and a steward came in, carrying a tray high. There were cups on the tray and two small pots, with a tag dangling from each on the end of a string. There was sugar in a bowl and a silverish pitcher. There was also a covered plate. "Down there, man," Whitney

123

said and gestured, and the steward put the tray down on the chest of drawers. He said, "Signor?"

"All right," Whitney said, and the steward said, "*Grazie,* signor," and went out. Whitney lifted the cover from the plate and said, "Scones, I give you my word," and put the cover back on again. "What they call scones, anyway. Have to let it steep, what? Still won't be tea, you know. Bags. Want one of those scones, Inspector?" He held the plate out. Heimrich didn't especially want a scone. He took one. He took a napkin which was held out to him and put the napkin down on a small table within reach and put the scone on it. Whitney lifted the lid of one of the teapots and looked into the pot and jiggled the tea bag up and down in it. He raised the lid of the silverish pot and looked into it and then held his hand against the metal. He said, "Warm. I'll give them that."

"You said something about Sir Ronald," Heimrich said. "I gathered something you wanted to tell me about him."

"Good man, Grimes," Whitney said. "Gather he's turned up missing. And that you're trying to find him. Won't, you know."

"I may not," Heimrich said. "Who told you he's missing, Major?"

"All over the ship," Whitney said. "Steward told me first, matter of fact. Their cabins are a couple of doors aft, y'know. Serves them too. But it's all over the ship. First class, anyway."

"I suppose it is," Heimrich said. "What did you want to tell me, Major?"

"Barged in on Lady Grimes this afternoon," Whitney said. "Sympathy. That sort of thing. Only thing to do, wouldn't you say?"

"A considerate thing to do," Heimrich said. "I take it you and the Grimeses are good friends?"

"Wouldn't go that far," Whitney said. "He was commercial at the Embassy, y'know. I'm on the military side. Not much contact, actually. But got to know him, and Ellen too. Even

124

took her to dinner once or twice when he was tied up. Played tennis with her a few times. He was past that, y'know."

"He was, I take it, around sixty," Heimrich said. "A good many men of sixty play tennis."

"Not Grimes," Whitney said. "What I'm getting at. Ellen didn't know, and there you are."

Heimrich didn't see that he was anywhere. Whitney looked again into the teapot and bounced the tea bag in it again. "Good as it's going to get," he said, and poured from the pot into one of the cups. He said, "Milk? Sugar?"

"Just as it is," Heimrich said, and took the cup held out to him and put it down on the little table beside the scone. Whitney poured tea into the other up and added warm milk. He tasted from his cup and shook his head and put it down.

"What didn't Lady Grimes know?" Heimrich said and let patience sound in his voice.

"Getting to that," Whitney said. "I was pretty sure. Kind of a man he was, y'know. When I barged in on her this afternoon I—well, I sort of edged around it, y'know. She didn't have an inkling. I'd swear to that. She's got it all wrong, I think. And, I think you have, Heimrich."

"Major," Heimrich said, "if you've got something to tell me about Sir Ronald, tell me."

He let the patience drain out of his voice.

"All right," Whitney said. "No use edging around it with you, what? You think somebody killed Grimes. Pushed him over the side. And you've let Ellen think that. And you're wrong, y'know. Thought you ought to know."

Merton Heimrich closed his eyes. After a moment he opened them and looked at the resolutely handsome face opposite and said, "Know what, Major?"

"Grimes was washed up," Whitney said. "And knew it. Talked about going home and growing roses, but knew he wasn't going to. End of the line and knew it. End of a career —pretty satisfactory career, matter of fact. His whole life,

125

y'know. Put out to pasture, and knew there wasn't going to be any pasture. Know what I mean?"

"No. You're talking in circles."

"Don't mean to be. Damn it, man, he didn't want people to know. Sort of thing one doesn't like to do. Telling what people want kept secret. Didn't tell Ellen, matter of fact. Wouldn't have been the thing."

Heimrich sighed, making a good deal of it.

"All right. Grimes was a sick man. Had maybe six months to go. Not pleasant months. So, you can't blame him, can you? What I'd do myself, I shouldn't wonder."

"I take it." Heimrich said, "you're saying—trying to say—that Sir Ronald took his own life. That it, Major?"

"Couldn't be clearer, I'd think," Whitney said. He lighted a cigarette. "Inoperable. At the end of the line, it came to. Add them up. Retired to nothing. Six months to go. No good to anybody, probably the way he looked at it. No good to his country. No good to himself. And an ocean and a rail anybody could climb over."

"He told you he was sick? I take it it was cancer?"

"Not me," Whitney said. "Colonel Collins. My chief at the Embassy, the colonel is. They were old friends. Grimes and the colonel, I mean. Family sort of thing. Went back for generations, in a way of speaking. Always army, the Grimeses were. Except Ronald himself. Anyway, he told Collins, and the colonel—well, he let it leak. Broken up, the colonel was. Friends for years, y'know."

"Let it leak to you, I take it?"

"Didn't mean to, probably. As I said, he was broken up. Yes. To me, Heimrich."

"To others?"

"I wouldn't know."

"When was this? That you learned about Sir Ronald's illness?"

"Two-three months ago."

"And you think that, knowing he was going to die, Sir Ronald committed suicide?"

"That, and the fact that he was being put out to pasture. Yes. Rather jumps out at one, wouldn't you say?"

Heimrich closed his eyes again. He opened them and sipped from his cup. The tea was all right, as tea went. It was no longer especially hot.

"It could have been that way," he said. "It's—it's something I'll bear in mind, Major. Did you know a man named Hunt?"

Whitney merely repeated the name. Then he shook his head.

"Lady Grimes didn't say anything about him?"

Whitney shook his head again.

"The same night Sir Ronald disappeared," Heimrich said, "a man named Hunt was murdered. Detective Inspector Albert Hunt. English. Assigned to the Special Branch. You never heard of him?"

"Can't say I have, Inspector. Special Branch, you say?"

"Yes." He waited a moment. Whitney merely shook his head. "Wasn't around the Embassy the last few weeks? Or months?"

"Now there you've got me. Could have been, I suppose. Good many people in and out. Rather a busy place. If he was, I never ran into him. Afraid I don't get the connection, Inspector."

"Between Sir Ronald's disappearance and Inspector Hunt's murder? The same night?"

"Coincidence," Ian Whitney said. "Sure to have been, I'd think. This Hunt. He was a copper, you say? Good many people have it in for coppers. Good many people in this ship. Wander all over it, actually. Come up from tourist if they don't believe in signs. After somebody on the ship? And somebody got there first?"

He put out the cigarette he had been smoking and lighted another. Then, unexpectedly, he smiled. It didn't change his

127

face as much as smiles change most faces, Heimrich thought.

"Matter of fact," Whitney said, "friend of mine aboard. Pretty little thing. Cabin class but I've had her up for drinks once or twice."

"Small," Heimrich said. "Very pretty. Black hair."

"That's Sylvia," Whitney said. "Sylvia Blake. Nice kid. American but a nice kid. Met her in Washington. And getting out of a cab at the pier. So I looked her up, what? Aboard ship, I mean. Going to look her up again in Venice, shouldn't wonder."

Heimrich stood up. He said, "Thanks for telling me about Sir Ronald, Major. Probably be helpful."

"Thought I ought to," Whitney said, and stood up too and went with Heimrich to the door of the cabin.

Going down in an elevator to the upper deck, Heimrich remembered he hadn't eaten his scone. He also wondered whether Major Ian Whitney was always so long in getting to his point. He had no way of knowing. There was nobody he could ask about Major Whitney. Oh, of course, there was one person. A person who was looking out at an empty world through the shock in her eyes. Or, of course, perhaps was doing that. If she really was in shock.

There was one other person. Heimrich made his way back up to the wireless room on the sun deck and put through another call to the British Embassy. He found out, in spite of a certain amount of static, that Colonel Collins was away from Washington and would not return until next week.

ૐ 10

Heimrich went into Cabin 82 as quietly as he could. Susan was in her bed, but she was not asleep. She looked up at him. She did not ask any questions. She merely looked at him. She knows his face and can see answers in it to questions she has not asked. Heimrich sat on his own bed and looked across the cabin at her.

"Nothing that proves anything," he said. "Whitney took Lady Grimes to dinner once or twice when Grimes was tied up. Played tennis with her a few times, because Grimes wasn't up to tennis. What he wanted to tell me, apparently. What Grimes wasn't up to. That Grimes was a sick man, pretty close to a dying man. But, still active enough to climb over a ship's rail and jump overboard. Because it was a quicker way to die. And that Grimes had not told his wife how sick he was."

"How would he know that? Whitney, I mean?"

"I don't know. He may be wrong, naturally. Wrong about Sir Ronald's sickness, come to that. He got it secondhand. But —he may be right, of course. A sick man. And a man thrown

129

out of his job. His whole life, Whitney says Grimes's career was to him. And that could be true."

Susan sat up in bed and continued to look across the cabin at Merton Heimrich. Then she shook her head. Then she said, "Merton, if you were sick—really sick, fatally sick—would you try to keep it from me?"

"No," he said. "I don't try to keep things from you."

"Because anyway you couldn't," she said. "I think Sir Ronald and Ellen Grimes were the way we are. Something the way we are. You thought so too."

"Yes," he said. "But that's not good enough, is it? What we guess at about people? Only, this is pretty much all guesswork with nothing—damn it, with nothing to base anything on."

"Whitney thinks Sir Ronald committed suicide," Susan said. "Says he does, anyway. And what about Hunt? Is he supposed to have strangled himself?"

"Coincidence," Heimrich said. "That Hunt was a policeman. That he may have been after somebody on the ship. That whoever he was after got to him first." He paused. He closed his eyes. "This ship goes to Trieste, doesn't it?" he said, without opening them. "After we get off her?"

"The last port," Susan said. "Then she turns around and goes back. Why?"

"Trieste is close to Yugoslavia," Heimrich said. "Which is close to Hungary. Not a member of the club, Yugoslavia isn't. Not in good standing, anyway. But—there may be holes in the curtain there. And—people to widen holes. I wonder where the Grimeses planned to leave the ship."

Susan merely shook her head. But then she stopped shaking it and looked at him silently for some moments, and then she said, "Oh," with a falling inflection. Then she said, "I don't believe it, Merton."

"People do defect," he said. "Oh both sides, to both sides. And—efforts are made to stop them. Hush-hush efforts, to avoid the stirring up of messes. Making scandal."

"You look tired," Susan said. "You're supposed to look rested."

"Frustrated," Heimrich said. "A day of getting nowhere."

"Then call it a day. There'll be tomorrow."

He shook his head and stood up. He said there were not too many days before Monday and Málaga. He looked at her a little anxiously. "Are you all right, Susan?"

"I'm fine," she said. "But if it's Lady Grimes—to ask whether they had planned to go through to Trieste—I don't think you'll find her alone. I'm pretty sure she went to tea in the main lounge with Miss Farrell."

Heimrich looked his question.

"I got to thinking of her being alone," Susan said. "I couldn't bear it for her, Merton—the awful waiting." She drew a breath. "I went up to her cabin. And Miss Farrell had the same thought, I guess—she was already there, and she had Lady Grimes at least half-persuaded to go to tea. So I came back. And I don't believe for a minute—"

Heimrich tipped Susan's face up to his. He smiled down at her. He said, "I'll just go and make sure."

He went above to the promenade deck and stood in the entrance to the lounge—the wide entrance through which they had been ushered to the officers' cocktail party. (They had fled it through the entrance across the ship.)

There were a good many people in the lounge having tea—tea and little sandwiches and little cakes. Most of the people were women. At first he did not see Miss Farrell and Ellen Grimes. Then, across the big room, he saw them, at a table wedged among other tables. A steward was pouring into their cups. Lady Grimes was not looking at the steward, or at Emily Farrell. She did not appear to be looking at anyone.

She was still a very pretty woman, as she sat not looking at anyone. But then, as he watched, she seemed to focus on Miss Farrell. And she smiled and said something. She was dressed in black, but it was not really the black of mourning, because there was a broad red belt around her waist. The "little black

131

dress" all women have. The red belt probably was integral to it. After dinner, he thought. But we should dance after dinner; we are on holiday. All right, after dinner.

He went out on deck and stood looking at the horizon, running things through his mind.

Whether her husband had told her, or she had learned without being told, that he was gravely sick—that he was close to dying. Whether, in the last few weeks, or few months, he had seemed depressed. Whether being retired, having his career finished, had eaten into him. And whether they had planned to go on in *Italia* to Trieste, which was so close to Yugoslavia. Whether their passports were visaed for Yugoslavia, if a visa was required there, as he supposed it was. Whether Sir Ronald Grimes, Bart., descendant of a long line of baronets, had planned to defect to the East.

Those were questions to be asked of Lady Ellen Grimes. (The last, of course, not in so many words.) And whether Grimes had had an attaché case, as would become a diplomat, and whether it was still in the other cabin of their suite. And—

He went down to the upper deck and to Cabin 82. Susan did not appear to be in it, and for a moment he felt a twinge of alarm. Which was absurd. She was—

He went to the door of the bathroom and listened. She was having her shower. He went back into the main room and pushed his shoes off and lay down on his bed.

Susan came from the bathroom into the cabin. She came quietly. She also came naked. She said, "Oh, I didn't know you were back. I suppose I should have worn a robe."

He looked up at her. After a moment he said, "Why?"

"Come to think of it," Susan Heimrich said, "I haven't the least idea."

Merton Heimrich took his turn in the shower. They dressed. (Heimrich had less trouble with his black tie; he was getting used to it.) They went up to the *veranda belvedere*, and Mario said, "Madam, sir," with gladness in his voice. (Ten dollars their last night aboard? Heimrich wondered.) Mario brought their drinks. (I'm really drinking too much, Susan thought. I should have ordered a small glass of very dry sherry.) She said, "Thank you, Mario," for a not especially small glass of very dry martini.

The room was more nearly filled than it had been on earlier evenings. The four Frenchmen were at their usual table, and their voices were still loud. Mrs. Raymond Powers was in the lounge. She was not, this time, alone at a table. She was sitting on one of the small sofas with the black-haired girl beside her —Major Whitney's very pretty black-haired girl—and the major sat on a chair facing them.

The silver-white streak through Lucinda Powers's hair was even more strikingly clear than usual. "The hairdressers are good on this ship," Susan said. "Mrs. Powers hasn't worn that dress before. Isn't the major's girl pretty?"

"Sylvia Blake her name is," Merton told his wife. "She's in cabin class. He brings her up."

"Understandably," Susan said. "They make a fine-looking couple." She turned suddenly to Merton. "But then," she said, "so do we, I think."

"Half of one. Your half. I—"

"If you say that again," Susan told him, "or anything like that, I'll—probably throw my drink at you."

Ellen Grimes was not in the lounge. Heimrich had not supposed she would be. She had ventured out for tea. Probably she had fled back to lonely refuge. But I don't know a damn thing about her, he thought. She may be in the main cocktail lounge pouring down Scotches. He glanced at Susan and decided he was probably wrong.

Music suddenly burst loudly into the room. The men in red jackets—the men with a guitar and a violin and a tenor voice—had arrived. They went from table to table and played and sang at each, and they were, Susan thought, rather loud about it. And, of course, extremely Italian, which was appro-

133

priate. They stopped at the Heimrich's table, and the man with the voice said, "Signor? Signora?"

"Can you do 'Forget Domani?'" Susan asked him. "The way Frank Sinatra does?"

"Ah," the tenor said. "The Sinatra. The great Sinatra. But of course, signora."

The violin and the guitar went at something with gusto; the tenor sang in Italian, with a yearn in his voice. But it was not "Forget Domani," and it was not in the least like Frank Sinatra.

The music moved on to the far side of the room which spanned the breadth of the ship. It became dance music, and Whitney and the black-haired girl and two other couples danced to it on the circular floor. Mario brought another round of drinks. The tenor sang something which Merton Heimrich found faintly operatic, and the dancers left the floor and went back to their tables. After what seemed to Susan a rather long time, and a rather noisy time, the dinner chimes sounded.

The four Frenchmen rose as one. Merton and Susan finished their drinks and followed the Frenchmen. Lucinda Powers was moving toward the wide doorway. The musicians reverted to dance music, and Whitney and his black-haired girl danced again, but this time they danced alone on the oval floor.

Half a bottle of Soave Bolla was on the Heimrichs' table. There was roast prime rib of beef on the menu, which has a homey sound and which could, yes, be served rare. Lorenzo looked at the wine bottle and said, "The wine steward, signor?" and Heimrich, though remembering that reds went with beef, shook his head. "A little pâté," Susan said. "And the veal pepperoni, please."

At the adjacent table, with her three companions of chance, Miss Emily Farrell had reached minestrone, and seemed to be enjoying it. But when Lorenzo had left, she looked at the

134

Heimrichs, and her face suddenly became very sad. "She did come to tea," she said to Susan. "That's something the English just naturally do, I guess. But she wasn't going to want dinner, she said. Poor girl."

"I'm glad you were with her," Susan said. "I'm sure it helped."

"I do hope so." Miss Farrell went back to minestrone.

"We can sit on the deck," Susan said. "The enclosed deck. There's a moon, I think."

She looked up at him.

"No," she said, "I didn't think so, really. I'll write a letter to Michael. I'll send cards to some other people. I'll send a card to the vet and ask about our animals."

It was a hell of a holiday, Heimrich thought, and went down to the cabin with Susan. There was writing paper—"Aboard S.S. Italia"—in a drawer, and there were postcards with pictures of *Italia* steaming through unruffled seas. Heimrich used the telephone, and the stewardess answered. Yes, Lady Grimes was in her cabin. But she was just finishing dinner. If Inspector Heimrich—

There was a momentary pause. Then the voice was Ellen Grimes's voice. She said, "Inspector?" and for a moment it seemed to Heimrich there was hope in her voice.

"No, Lady Grimes. Just a few things I'd like to ask you."

She said, "Oh," in a voice with no hope in it. She said, "Of course, Inspector. Come when you like."

The stewardess was carrying a tray out of Cabin 18 when Heimrich went along the passageway. She drew aside to let him pass. She said, "Signor Inspector. She is waiting for you, the poor lady. Of her dinner she did not eat, except only a little. A very little, the poor lady."

Ellen Grimes was sitting where she had sat before when he had gone to the cabin. She wore a robe belted tightly about her waist. Her lips, he thought, were very pale. She had not used lipstick. Her eyes were large, and there were

135

shadows under them. The door which opened on the adjacent
—empty—room was closed. She looked up at him, and for a
moment there was, he thought, a flicker of hope, of expec-
tancy, in her eyes. But he did not need even to shake his head.
She looked at his face, and the flicker died out of her eyes.

"I went to tea," she said. "It was so good of Miss Farrell
—and of your wife to think of me, too. But I'm all right,
really." Her voice was very steady. "Can I have them bring you
something? Coffee? A drink?"

"No," Heimrich said. "I won't bother you long, Lady
Grimes. Only one or two things. To clarify a point or two."

"You're still working on it? Haven't—haven't found out
what happened?"

"Yes," Heimrich said. "Still working on it, Lady Grimes. I
hope we—the captain's men and I—will find out something
before you leave the ship."

"At Lisbon," she said. "Michael—my stepson Michael—
is meeting me there. Sir Michael Grimes, ninth baronet. There
isn't any real doubt of that, is there?"

On her stepson's name her voice had shaken a little. Then
it had become firm again.

"I shouldn't have asked that," she said. "Asked you to answer that. We're flying to England, Michael and I. They've
given him leave, of course. Compassionate leave, they call
it. Such heavy words, they use. Such formal words. They—"

Her voice had broken again. She said, "I'm sorry, Inspector.
What do you want to ask me?"

"You and Sir Ronald," he said. "How far had you planned
to go on the ship?"

"To Venice, we'd decided. We were booked to Trieste.
Ronald was once a consul there. Years ago—oh, years ago.
But we—" Her voice broke again on the word "we." It
strengthened again at once. "We thought it might be spring
in Venice. Something like spring. And Venice can be lovely in
the spring. Do you know Venice, Inspector Heimrich?"

"No. We may—we've thought we may—stop there on our way home."

"There's a wonderful old church there," she said. "Hundred of years old—a thousand years old, perhaps. As it was a thousand years ago, I expect. Not in the city. On an island quite a way out in the harbor. They take you out in a launch. You arrange it at Harry's Bar, because the bar owns the restaurant on the island. A good restaurant, we—we always thought. It was rough the first time Ronald and I were there. Just a chop, really, but—but I almost got seasick. Which would have been bad, because it was our first—I'm sorry, Inspector. Only—I was afraid Ronald would be ashamed of me. I was wrong. I found out he was never like that. But—oh, people who are never sick themselves—"

She put both hands up to cover her face, and she shook her head, slowly. She spoke without moving her hands. "I'm miserably sorry to be like this," she said. "So ashamed to be like this."

"You have every reason to be," Heimrich said. "I know how you must feel—do feel. I'm the one to be sorry, Lady Grimes. But—well, we have to find out about things like this. We can't let them just happen. And the more we can learn—"

She took her hands down. She said, "I'll be all right. It's just—oh, things coming back. Actually, I want to help. Desperately want to help."

He held a pack of cigarettes out to her and, when she took a cigarette out of it, lighted it for her and lighted one of his own. She said, "I'm all right now. The things you wanted to ask me?"

"You say your husband was never sick," Heimrich said. "You mean, when he was younger?"

"He was always well, Inspector. Why do you ask that?"

"Recently? The last year or so?"

"Of course. Inspector, he wasn't an old man. He was—oh, he was just over sixty. That isn't old for people nowadays.

137

Not really old. Ronald—Ronald was—do you ask because he was so thin? But he was always thin. Always since I've known him."

She smiled. It was not much of a smile, but it was a try at a smile.

"You should have seen him play tennis," she said. "If you've got the notion he was a frail old man."

"Recently?"

"Last summer. Into the early fall. Washington has good autumns, sometimes. He was all *right*, Inspector. He was never sick. Why do you ask about that?"

"Because," Heimrich said, "somebody's told me he wasn't well. That he was very sick, actually."

"Who told you that? Wait—Mrs. Powers? She didn't like Ronald. She had some—oh, some mad idea—that he was, somehow, responsible for her husband's death. She's—well, she's rather odd, Inspector. Was it Mrs. Powers?"

"No. Major Whitney."

"Ian? But why would he say a thing like that?"

"I don't know. He seemed to think it was true. And that —well, that your husband had never let you know how sick he was."

"I don't know what's come over Ian. He's—I wouldn't have thought he'd say anything like that. He hardly knew Ronald. Oh, they were both at the Embassy. But doing very different things, y'know."

"You knew Major Whitney better than your husband did?"

"Not really. Once or twice, when Ronald was tied up, I had dinner with him. At the club. Oh, I played tennis with him a few times. At the club. When Ronald was tied up with a men's double match. Once I beat him, too. Took him down a peg, I shouldn't wonder. And now—now he's making up these absurd stories."

Heimrich waited because he thought she planned to go on. After a few moments she did.

138

"He should have lived for years," she said. "The men in his family always lived for years. Always. And he was looking forward to living back at the old place. And growing roses. Roses, he always said. Or cabbages. Saying that was—was a kind of joke with him. There is a kitchen garden, of course. But he—he so loved flowers. He—I'm getting maudlin, aren't I? I never thought I would be like this."

"Looking forward to retirement," Heimrich said. "Not—oh, at loose ends because he was retired? Not feeling that his life was ended?"

She said, "Ended?"

"Some men who are retired can't adjust to it," Heimrich said. "Feel put on a shelf. Or out to pasture. However you'd phrase it."

"Not Ronald," she said. "Never Ronald." The words came quickly. Then, for some seconds, she looked at him. Her voice was very steady, very level, when she spoke again.

"What did Ian Whitney tell you?" she said. "What did he make you think—try to make you think? That my husband was an old, sick man? A man come to the end of his tether? Is that what Ian told you?"

"What he seemed to think," Heimrich said. "Yes."

She moved as if she were about to stand up. But instead she leaned forward and put both hands down flat on the table in front of her.

"And—and that Ronald might have killed himself? Is that what you're getting at?"

"What Whitney was, yes."

"I don't understand. I don't understand at all. Why would he say things like that?"

"I don't know, Lady Grimes. He seemed quite convinced."

Again she looked at him for some seconds without speaking. When she spoke, it was in the same level voice.

"My husband loved being alive," she said. "Alive with me. I don't know why Ian Whitney would—" She did not finish the sentence. She said, "What time is it, Inspector?"

139

It was a little after nine.

"It's earlier in Washington, isn't it," she said. She did not say it as a question, but Heimrich nodded his head. She said, he thought to herself, "He keeps late hours, sometimes," and got up and walked across to the telephone. After a moment's wait she said, "This is Lady Grimes in Cabin Eighteen. I want to make a call to Washington. Washington, D.C. To Dr. Arnold Oliver. The number is—" She gave a number. She said, "Very well, if you will," and cradled the telephone. She went back to where she had been sitting.

"He examined Ronald in January," she said. "We both had checkups in January. He won't talk to you unless I ask him to, of course. They'll call back if they can get through to him."

When she moved, Heimrich thought, she moved directly, with decision. Whether Dr. Arnold Oliver would discuss a patient even when asked by the patient's wife—or widow—was an open question. It would be interesting if he would.

"While we're waiting," Heimrich said, "did your husband have an attaché case, do you know?"

"Yes," she said. "Flat. Dark green. It's—"

Her voice broke for an instant. But then she went on, her voice again steady.

"It's in there," she said, and pointed toward the closed door to the next cabin. "All his things are there. I'll have to have the steward pack them up before Lisbon, I suppose. I—I waited. I—I knew it wasn't any good waiting, but I waited. I—it was just putting it off, wasn't it? Just pushing it away?"

Heimrich didn't answer that, because the only answer would be "Yes," and that wouldn't be any good either.

"I'd like to look at his things, Lady Grimes. I might find something that would help."

She said, "Of course. The door isn't locked. It—it was never locked."

He went into the next cabin, leaving the door open behind him. It was a little smaller than Cabin 18. There was a closet with two suits hanging in it, both dark suits, and a sports jacket and slacks beside it and a Burberry and a terry-cloth robe. All the clothes were hung neatly on their hangers.

There were two suitcases in the luggage area. One had seen considerable use; the other appeared to be new. There was also a flat green attaché case. Heimrich was a little surprised to find it still there. It would be locked, of course. Yes, it had a combination lock. Conceivably, Ellen Grimes might know the combination. Probably she would not. Probably—

He put the case down on the bed and started to twirl the inset combination wheel and found that, under his finger, it spun with no resistance. As if—

He looked more closely. The leather around the lock was scored. A knife blade, probably. He lifted the lid of the case, and it rose without resistance. And the case was empty.

A forced lock, which would not have been difficult. A lock Sir Ronald himself would not, of course, need to have forced. Unless he had some reason to want it to appear that the case had been forced open? What reason? To involve some unknown person, and so to refute a theory of suicide if such a theory were to be advanced?

It was conceivable. It was also far-fetched.

He went through drawers in a chest, and found shirts and socks and handkerchiefs and other things which one might expect to find. He did not find papers, incriminating or not incriminating, which might have been taken from the attaché case.

Fingerprints on the attaché case? His own, now. Probably Sir Ronald's. But he had no equipment to take fingerprints or lift them, and probably the security force of *Italia* hadn't either. And he could not remember that fingerprints had ever been of much use in the cases he had handled. One merely missed the familiarity of routine.

The two suitcases were empty. So were the pockets of the

neatly hanging suits and sports jacket. Sir Ronald Grimes had not been a man to stuff his pockets. Whatever he had needed to carry with him had been, presumably, in pockets of the dinner clothes he was wearing and if so, now at the bottom of—

The telephone rang in the next cabin. Probably the operator to tell Lady Grimes Dr. Arnold Oliver was not—

"Arnold," Ellen Grimes said. "It is Arnold? A most dreadful thing has happened. Ronald has—has disappeared. Yes, from the ship. We—we don't know, Arnold. They're—they're trying to find out."

For some seconds then she did not speak. Then she said, "I know you do, Arnie. And I know there isn't anything to say. Listen. Maybe you can't. I know that. But there's a man here—a police inspector who just happened to be aboard and is trying to help—somebody's told him Ronald was sick. Very sick. Will you talk to him? Tell him—oh, anything you can? Will you do that?"

Heimrich was in the room by then. She held the receiver out to him, and he took it, and she went back to sit where she had before.

Heimrich said, "Doctor? My name's Heimrich. Yes, a policeman. New York State Police. No official standing here, except the ship's captain—"

He was interrupted. The voice which interrupted him was deep, and static marred it little.

"Sir Ronald's disappeared. That's what Ellen's been telling me?"

"Yes. He seems not to be on the ship. It's been searched. The inference is—"

"I know what the inference is. Lady Grimes? She's—making do?"

"Very well, under the circumstances, Doctor. Very bravely."

"Expect it of her," Dr. Oliver said. "Got guts, that one. Who told you Sir Ronald was sick?"

142

"A man aboard. A man who knew him."

"Nothing to it. Not a damn thing to it, man. Fit as they come, Ronald was. Not as young as he was once, but who the hell is? What did this man you say knew him tell you was the matter with Ronald Grimes? Because whoever told you he was sick is a jackass. Not a doctor, is he?"

"No. He wasn't specific. Said he'd got it all secondhand. He implied cancer. Near terminal stage. You examined Sir Ronald recently, Lady Grimes tells me?"

"January," Oliver said. "Annual checkup. Good about that. They both were, long as I've known them."

"He didn't have cancer?"

"Didn't have anything. Oh, that's not true, of course. Everybody's got something. Particularly at sixty. Start of emphysema, probably. But who hasn't who's lived all his life in cities? Nothing conclusive in the picture. Just suspicious. Told him to give up smoking. Had to watch what he ate, to a degree. Touchy stomach. Worked too hard, too many years, too much strain. Chronic gastritis."

"You ran a G.I. series on him?"

"Obviously. And an electrocardiogram. Perfectly sound heart. Perfectly sound man, or as close as he had any right to be. And what's this got to do with the fact that he's disappeared?"

"I don't precisely know, Doctor," Heimrich said, "I'm trying to find out."

"All right," Dr. Oliver said. "Like to speak to Ellen. Put her on again, will you?"

"Yes," Heimrich said, and held the telephone toward Ellen Grimes and beckoned with it. She came across the cabin slowly and took the telephone. Heimrich went back into the other cabin. There are times when there really isn't anything to say. Those are the times when people insist on saying it.

Dr. Arnold Oliver would make consoling sounds to Ellen Grimes. A friend of hers, as well as her physician, Heimrich

143

judged from the way she had spoken. She would make responding sounds. The pattern, the meaningless pattern, would be completed. Heimrich looked out through one of the windows of Cabin 16. Susan had been right about the moon; there was moonlight on the water. It rippled with the water, swelled with the water. But the moon was on the other side of the ship. Its light just touched the ship's rail, leaving the deck in darkness except for lights burning at intervals in the overhead. If they had gone to sit in their chairs on the enclosed deck, they would not have sat in moonlight.

Heimrich looked again into the empty attaché case. It was as empty as it had been before. It was not new; in a corner the lining had a small rent in it. Heimrich put a finger in behind the torn lining. The finger found nothing. The two suitcases still were empty. The pockets of the two suits were empty, and the pockets of the sports jacket—

Wait a minute, he told himself. Above the right-hand jacket pocket there was a small, separate pocket with its own flap. A change pocket, presumably. Or a pocket merely considered ornamental. In any case, a pocket he had overlooked before. He ran a finger into it; there was room for only one of his fingers. A silly little pocket in a well-cut jacket.

His probing finger encountered something in the pocket. A match folder, it felt like. He fished it out. It was a match folder with the words "Field and Tennis" lettered on it. About half the matches had been torn out. The Washington club at which Ronald Grimes had played tennis, probably. A match folder dropped casually into a useless little pocket. Heimrich opened the folder. Somebody had used the flap as a note pad.

The penciled notes were written very small, in a tight hand. Heimrich switched on a light on the dressing table and could make out the words, or almost make them out. "A. Schmidt Gesel." Or what looked like that. "Zrinjevac 48 Zag." Or what looked like that. The address of somebody named "Gesel.?"

144

Or—wait a minute—of a company. "A. Schmidt Gesell-schaft?" It might be that. In something called "Zag.?" It looked like "Zag." in the cramped writing. An abbreviation for—for what? Heimrich riffled through his mind and found nothing useful. Unless—

Zagreb. Wasn't there a city somewhere named that? A very ancient city? In—wait a minute. Riffle another of the mind's pages. Yugoslavia. That was it. Near Trieste? There was no use riffling the mind for that. It wouldn't be there. It would be in an atlas, if *Italia*'s library contained an atlas. Which it probably didn't.

Heimrich carried the match folder back into the adjacent cabin. Ellen Grimes was sitting at the dressing table, and the telephone was in its cradle. She turned and looked at him, and her young face seemed to sag. She pulled it back together. She did not say anything.

Heimrich held the match folder down to her, his finger pointing to what was written inside the flap. He waited while she read it and until she looked up again at him.

"Does it mean anything to you, Lady Grimes?" Heimrich asked her.

She shook her head slowly. Then she said, "Nothing, In-spector."

"Is it your husband's handwriting?"

She looked at it again.

"It's written so small," she said. "Not the way he wrote. It doesn't look like his writing. But—I suppose it might be, if—whoever wrote it was cramped for space. I don't know, Inspector."

She tucked the flap back in.

"It's from the club," she said. "His club. The—the club where we played."

⚘ 11

Heimrich walked slowly forward through the lighted passageway. Sir Ronald Grimes had been dying of cancer; he had been depressed because his career was ended. He had had nothing more wrong with him than apparently minor indigestion. He had been looking forward to a reasonable number of years of life and to the cultivation of his garden. A doctor vouched for his health. With more frankness than doctors usually show in talking of the patients? A doctor who was, apparently, a fairly close friend of Lady Ellen Grimes's. Was Ian Whitney another friend? A closer one than she now admitted?

It added to nothing certain. An attaché case which had been forced open and left empty. Another attaché case which, if it had existed, had disappeared. Papers in either which might incriminate someone? Or extra pairs of shorts and socks? A match folder with what might be the address of a German firm penciled in it. A German firm—Schmidt was certainly German enough but, come to that, so was Heimrich—in a place which might be Zagreb, Yugoslavia. And might not.

The ship's small library was on this deck. He could see if it contained an atlas on its shelves. He would—

He came to an exit to the deck. Fresh air might blow something into his mind, which could do with having something blown into it. He went out to the deck. He could walk around outside the *veranda belvedere* and go back in on the port side and have a look at the library. The writing room was across a passageway from the library. Susan might have gone there to write her letters and postcards. On the other hand—his watch said ten minutes of eleven—she probably would have gone below by now. He would just have a look.

It was cool on the open deck, and there was a breeze. It was not enough to disturb the ocean, which moved under the moonlight in easy swells. Heimrich started forward toward the prow of *Italia* and the balcony which circled in front of the *veranda belvedere*. And a sound made him turn.

It was a soft thumping sound, and after it there was another, heavier, thumping sound. Then, as he looked down the deck, he saw a rapidly receding shadow. And he heard the sound of someone running—running aft down the deck, away from Heimrich. Then, between him and the running shadow, he heard what sounded like a moan.

He ran along the dimly lighted deck toward the moaning sound. The running shadow vanished in front of him—was a flicker of movement, then disappeared. In the brief glimpse he had had of it, it had never been more than a shadow—a shadow almost shapeless, of no height, no dimension. And it had merged with, vanished into, the ship's shadow.

What was lying on the ship's deck did not vanish. It was a man, or the body of a man. Heimrich crouched beside it. A slight man, wearing a steward's uniform, lying face downward on the deck. And—breathing. Breathing slowly, with evident effort, but breathing.

And blood was flowing from the back of his head, matting dark hair. The wound was straight and narrow and looked

147

deep. It was, Heimrich thought, such a wound as a narrow club might make; such a wound as a thin walking stick might make. But there was no time now to wonder about the wound.

Heimrich lifted the man in his arms, and the man bled on him. His run aft had taken him roughly admidships, and a few yards beyond was an entry door into the ship. The door was heavy, tightly closed. It opened outward toward the deck. Heimrich had to lower the bleeding man so that his feet rested on the deck and hold him there with an arm around his waist and tug at the heavy door. It opened with reluctance. It tried to close itself again. Heimrich got his back against it and braced it open and lifted the man over the high sill, and the door pushed him into the ship. He picked the slight man up again in his arms.

At the passageway, Heimrich turned right and was opposite a door numbered 18. That was Lady Grimes's cabin. The next cabin was empty—now it was empty. He could not carry a man—a man who might be dying—down many stairways to the hospital on A deck. The next cabin—

A steward was coming down the passageway toward Heimrich, and when he saw what Heimrich was carrying in his arms, he began to run. When he was a few feet away, he said, "Hurt. "He's hurt!" There was astonishment, disbelief, in his voice.

Heimrich had stopped in front of Cabin 16. He said, "In there," and the steward opened the door, and Heimrich carried the man into the room which had been Sir Ronald Grimes's and laid him on the bed. The wound still was bleeding, and the steward got towels from the bathroom and put them under the bleeding head.

"Get help," Heimrich said. "Get a doctor."

The steward picked up the telephone and dialed and then began to speak rapidly, in Italian.

The man's face was thin and young. It was almost a boy's

face. The boy had grown a thin, black mustache, which was still only a line across his upper lip.

He was still breathing with effort; his eyes were closed, and he seemed to fight for each breath. Heimrich pulled back jacket and shirt and put fingers against the boy's chest. The heart was beating, and it seemed to Heimrich to be beating regularly enough. But a layman can only guess about such things.

"They come," the steward said, standing behind Heimrich, who was bent over the boy. "At once they come. He fell, sì? Hit his head on something."

"I don't know," Heimrich said. "I think he was hit with something. You told them to hurry?"

"Sì, signor. That it was very bad and to hurry. His name is Louis, signor. His last name I do not know. He is new on the ship. Just learning the service, signor. On night duty. What we call caretaker duty. In English it is that, I think. He is young, signor. Will he die?"

And then the steward crossed himself.

"I don't know," Heimrich said. "It may be only a scalp wound. But—it may be anything. Contusion, obviously. Or a fractured skull."

"He is young, signor," the steward said. "The young can stand much."

Heimrich looked up at the steward. The steward was not young.

They had not closed the cabin door. A man in a white jacket came into the cabin and after him another. The second man carried a rolled stretcher under his arm. And after them another man came—an older man with a stethoscope in the pocket of his white jacket. The third man was the doctor who had expressed such confidence in the ship's refrigerating system.

The doctor went to the boy on the bed and used his steth-

149

oscope and said, "Mmmm." He turned the boy enough so that he could see the wound and, gently, he touched the boy's head near the wound. He looked at Heimrich and said, "It is not good, Signor Inspector. There may be a fracture. He should not be moved, but we must move him. Luigi."

The word was an order, and one of the men in white jackets said, "Sì, signor," and he and the other man lifted the boy named Louis onto the unrolled stretcher and, carefully, carried him out of the cabin.

"He'll make it?" Heimrich said to the doctor, and the doctor shrugged his shoulders and said, "We can hope, Signor Inspector." Then he went out of the cabin after the two orderlies and their buden.

They had taken with them the towels the cabin steward had put under the bleeding head. Blood had soaked through the towels onto, and into, the bed's cover. The steward looked at the stained bed for some seconds and then sighed deeply and looked at Heimrich.

"It was on the deck, signor? Where he fell? Or, as you say signor, was hit?"

"Yes."

"He was not supposed to be there, signor. At eleven they go on duty, the caretaker stewards. Two on each deck, signor. One for the starboard cabins. One for those on the port side."

"Regular assignments? I mean, serving the same cabins each night?"

"That is usual, signor."

"Do you know what deck Louis was assigned to? And on which side of the ship?"

The steward shrugged. His shrug almost matched that of the doctor. He completed it by spreading his hands. He added unnecessary words. "I do not know, signor. The chief steward. He assigns us."

150

There was no point in staying there looking at a bloodied bed. He wondered whether Lady Ellen Grimes, in the next cabin, had heard movement and voices. Heimrich was inclined to knock at her door and ask her but decided against it. If she was lucky, she was asleep. If she was wise she had taken something to make her sleep.

Heimrich went out of the cabin and along the passageway and out the door through which he had carried the boy named Louis, on his first voyage as a steward. The boy with, at a guess, his first mustache.

The moon had moved a little, or the ship had changed its course a little. Now the moonlight lay on half the wide promenade of the boat deck.

The shadow had moved aft and disappeared. Heimrich walked aft along the gently moving deck. He came to a door with "Classe Cabina" lettered on it and, below that lettering, "Cabin Class."

The door opened away from Heimrich. He pushed on it and it opened. He did not go through it.

The shadow could have gone through that door. It could have come through the door from cabin class and hit the steward and gone back the way it had come—become a shadow lost in shadows. The shadow of a man or of a woman? Heimrich had no way of being sure. The running footfalls had sounded like a man's—heavy, widely spaced. There had not —Heimrich thought there had not—been the click of a woman's heels. But not of a man's hard shoes either—only a hurried thudding.

Through the door to cabin class? Probably. But that did not mean that the shadow was traveling cabin class. It meant only that there had been a door to escape through.

Heimrich walked all the way forward and around the *veranda belvedere* to the port side and into the ship. The sounds of violin and guitar and tenor voice came out of the lounge.

151

Heimrich did not go into it. As he passed the writing room, he looked into it. It was empty. He had not really supposed that Susan had gone to it to write letters or postcards.

He went into the library with books behind glass doors on shelves. After a little time he found an atlas. Zagreb was in Yugoslavia. It appeared to be about a hundred miles from Trieste. It appeared to be about sixty miles from the Hungarian border. As a crow might fly. But all the many crows Heimrich had seen flew zigzag.

Starting out of the little library into the passageway, Heimrich had to step back to let a couple, bound for the lounge, pass him. They were people he did not remember having seen before. They looked at him, however, very intently, and the woman seemed to draw back, and she said, "Oh!" in a startled voice. But they went on into the lounge, and Heimrich went the other way and into an elevator and down to the upper deck.

He could use the telephone there and find out whether the boy who was growing his first mustache was going to live to go on with it. If they knew yet. He could use the telephone to find out to what deck, and to which side of the ship, the boy had been assigned the night before. Detective Inspector Hunt's cabin had been on the starboard side, as was the Heimrichs'. Had he seen something, or seen someone? You cannot ask questions of an unconscious man.

Guido was in the passageway near the door to Cabin 82. He said, "Good—" and stopped abruptly. He said, "*Signor* Inspector!" with an emphasis which surprised Heimrich, who said, "Evening, Guido," and went on into the cabin.

Susan was in her bed, reading. She turned toward him, and a smile started to form on her lips. But it died as it started, and she swung out of bed and stood, all in one swift motion, and came toward him and said. "Darling! *Merton!* You're hurt. Merton. *You're bleeding!*"

He remembered, then. He looked down at himself, at his

bloodied shirt. No wonder the couple on the boat deck had looked at him intently or that the woman had gasped an "Oh!" No wonder Guido had broken his "Good evening, signor" into bits.

"No, dear," Heimrich said to his wife. "Blood, yes. But not my blood, Susan. The blood of a man—a kid really—somebody tried to kill."

She sat down on her bed, and it was almost as if she had fallen onto it. Her breasts rose as she sucked air into her lungs. She let the air out as a sigh.

"Hit on the head," Heimrich said. "A steward. Who was on the boat deck near Lady Grimes's cabin. I found him. Carried him inside. He's in the hospital now."

"Dead? Someone else dead?"

"I don't know," Heimrich said. "Alive when they started down to the hospital with him. They were quick in coming."

He looked at his jacket. There was not much blood on it, or blood did not show so clearly on black fabric. He took the jacket off and the shirt, which was drenched with blood. "Hit on the head," Heimrich said and dropped the shirt on the desk. "Scalp wounds bleed like the devil."

Blood from the bleeding head had gone through the shirt onto Heimrich's chest.

"You'd better shower," Susan said. "And—wait a minute. I'll put the shirt in cold water." She started to stand up and then for a moment sank back and looked up at him. "You're all right?" she said. "You're really all right?"

Her voice shook a little.

"I'm fine," Heimrich said. "Getting nowhere, but getting there in one piece."

"Stay that way," Susan said and came off the bed and carried the shirt into the bathroom. She left the door open, and he could hear water running and then a sloshing sound. Susan came out after a few minutes. She said, "I don't know. They say cold water, but I don't know. Now you."

153

Merton Heimrich said, "Yes, lady," and went into the bathroom. There was some blood on his shorts, too. He put them into the wash basin with the shirt. The water in which the shirt was soaking was faintly red. He let the water out and ran fresh cold water and put shirt and shorts back in to soak. He doubted whether anything much was going to come of it.

He showered. Blood came off him all right. He was toweling when Susan came to the bathroom door and opened it.

"The telephone," Susan said. "Always in the middle of a shower, isn't it?"

He put a towel over his wide shoulders and, in the cabin, put it down on the dressing table bench to sit on. He still wasn't very dry. He said, "Heimrich," into the telephone.

"Ellen Grimes. I heard people moving in—in Ronald's cabin. And talking. I—I was half asleep. I—for a moment I thought—thought he'd come back. But I opened the door and—there wasn't anybody in the cabin. So he hasn't—"

"No, Lady Grimes. I wish it were another way. A man got hurt. We put him in there because it was the nearest place. He's in the hospital now."

"A man?"

Briefly he told her about the steward named Louis. She said, "Oh. How dreadful. This—this awful ship."

There wasn't anything to say to that. Heimrich made a sound to answer that.

"It wasn't about that I called you, Inspector," Ellen Grimes said. "Not really about that. I knew it wasn't that Ronald had come back. I—I was half asleep. I said that, didn't I? I—I dreamed he was moving in his cabin. That he would come in and we would have breakfast and—I'm not thinking straight, Inspector. My mind's all numbed. I didn't call you about that."

"I'm sorry it wasn't the way you dreamed, Lady Grimes," Heimrich said. "What did you call me about?"

"That match folder," Ellen Grimes said. "The one you showed me?"

"Yes?"

"I said I couldn't be sure whether the writing on it was Ronald's. But the more I think about it, the more sure I am it wasn't his. You found the match folder in his cabin?"

"Yes. In a pocket of his jacket. The little pocket in the right-hand side."

"That silly pocket," she said. "He never knew what was supposed to go in it. But—it doesn't make sense, Inspector."

"The pocket?"

"No. Matches being in it. Because Ronald didn't smoke, Inspector. Hadn't for a year. More than a year, actually. Arnold—Arnold Oliver, our doctor in Washington, told him the X-ray suggested emphysema, and that he'd better cut down on cigarettes. So Ronald quit them altogether. I—that's the way he does things, Inspector. The way—" There was a rather long pause. "The way he used to do things," Ellen Grimes said, and her voice was very steady. But it was also defeated. "Good night, Inspector." She hung up.

"Sir Ronald had a packet of matches in a jacket pocket," Heimrich said. "But he had given up smoking a year ago."

"Darling," Susan said, "she told us that at the captain's party. When she was saying how thin he was. Something about people being supposed to gain weight when they stopped smoking. Don't you remember?"

"No. Probably I didn't hear."

"Some men carry matches to light other people's cigarettes," Susan said. "At least, I knew one man who did. I'm almost sure I remember a man who did. It's almost midnight, isn't it? Since you're not hurt, I'm sleepy again."

"Yes," Heimrich said. "I am too, dear. A couple of calls first."

The steward named Louis—Louis Cataldi, he turned out to be—was still unconscious. Preliminary examination did not indicate a fracture. The concussion was severe. It might be hours before he regained consciousness. It might be days. And he might not remember, when he did, what had happened immediately before he lost consciousness.

Heimrich said, "Yes, Doctor. I know it happens that way."

He sighed because it did happen that way, which could be a way to a dead end.

He made another call.

Louis had been assigned to the upper deck, going on duty at eleven P.M. and staying on until seven. He had worked the starboard side of the ship. He had not, when he went off duty this morning, reported anything unusual having happened. Not to the chief steward, at any rate. What he might have said to other stewards nobody could guess.

"Ask Comandante Ferrancci's security people to ask around," Heimrich said. "In the morning."

He got a "Sì, Inspector," from whoever had answered the purser's telephone.

The Heimrichs went to bed.

⚒ 12

Sleep is supposed to refresh the mind. It is also supposed to knit up the raveled sleeve of care. At nine or thereabouts of Friday morning, Merton Heimrich could not find that it had done either of those things. Sleep had only increased the murk and enhanced his impatience with the whole muddled business. Angela and Guido brought breakfast, on trays held high. Guido looked at Heimrich with concern on his grave face. He said, "You are well, signor?"

"Quite well," Heimrich said. "Last night I had, er, merely spilled a drink on my shirt."

Some explanation was due. Guido said, "Sì, signor," with no conviction whatever in his voice.

"Not a very likely story," Susan said, across the cabin after the steward and stewardess had left.

"I was drinking a Bloody Mary," Heimrich told her. "The ship lurched."

They finished coffee. Heimrich lighted a cigarette. Lighting a cigarette, although he used a lighter, reminded him of a match folder. He got out of bed and got the match folder out

157

of the pocket of his dinner jacket and looked at it again. The penciled lines still said, "A. Schmidt Gesel. Zrinjevac 48 Zag." Put through another telephone call and listen, again, to static? This time, probably, in German, with which Heimrich is only mildly cognizant. Or Yugoslavian, which would be worse. Heimrich got back into bed and continued thinking that it was a hell of a holiday. Which reminded him.

"Are you all right?" he asked Susan. "It's being a hell of a trip for you."

"I'm fine," Susan said. "Really fine."

He got out of bed and crossed the room and looked down at her. She looked fine. She had already been up and put lipstick on and combed her short hair, still with the wave in it. She was meticulous about mornings. Heimrich ran fingers over his own face and decided he certainly needed to and went into the bathroom and shaved the face which needed it. He put on clothes—slacks and sport shirt and a sports jacket. He looked down at Susan and sighed.

"I know," she said. "Murder calls. No lazing on the deck."

"Tomorrow," Heimrich said. "Tomorrow and Sunday."

But he did not speak with any conviction.

"And Monday Spain," Susan said. "And this hotel in Nerja they told you about. And a balcony facing the Mediterranean. And lazing."

"The rain in Spain falls mainly," Heimrich said, and picked up the telephone and got at it.

Louis Cataldi was still unconscious. There was definitely no fracture. His pulse was almost normal; he was breathing satisfactorily. "A matter of time only, signor. We are quite certain of that." No, they could not predict how much time. Yes, they would notify the signor inspector when Louis Cataldi regained consciousness.

Another telephone call. Two men from the security force were questioning stewards to whom Louis might later have reported any strange occurrence on Wednesday night. The ones he would have been most likely to talk to would have been night stewards like himself. The signor inspector would understand that men assigned as night caretakers had breakfast and went to sleep after their tours were over. They were being waked up. The four who had been wakened could not remember that Louis had said anything. Louis had not, it appeared, been a boy who talked much. Of course, the signor inspector would understand, this was his first voyage in the *Italia*. He had not made many friends.

Heimrich put the telephone back in its cradle and looked at it with reproach. Telephones are poor substitutes for face-to-face conversation. And, of course, interrogation.

Louis, on duty between eleven o'clock Wednesday night and seven Thursday morning, would have gone back to the crew's quarters and had something to eat and gone to bed and to sleep. He would have been sleeping when Detective Inspector Albert Hunt's body had been found. He would not have heard of it until he had finished sleeping, probably in the late afternoon.

I should have looked him up then, Heimrich thought. Asked him then if he had seen anything out of the way. Or heard anything. Or the ship's security people should have. I can't be everywhere at once or even, apparently, think of everything at once. At home, routine would have taken care of that. Forniss would have taken care of that. At home, things move in order. Damn.

He said the last word aloud.

"Yes, darling," Susan said. "But it will all come clear."

He sighed an answer.

"After a while," Susan said, "I'll dress and go up on deck and—and read a book, perhaps. Is the sun shining?"

Heimrich crossed the room and looked out a porthole. The sun was shining. He told her the sun was shining.

"You'll find me on the deck then," Susan said. "Reading

159

a book. Drinking consommé. Come and find me when you can."

He leaned down and kissed her. He said, "Good morning, Susan." She said, "Good morning, darling."

She did not ask him where he would be, which was as well, since he had no notion. Probably on a telephone, talking fruitlessly ship to shore. Talking to people who would not answer. Or, come to that, call him back. A man named Parsons. Executive director of something called Continental Forwarding, Limited. A man who should have got a message asking him to call Inspector M. L. Heimrich aboard *Italia*. And who apparently hadn't, or had ignored it. Because if it was getting on toward ten aboard *Italia* it would be considerably later than that in London.

"Take care of yourself," Merton Heimrich told his wife. "I'm sorry things are this way."

"Spain," Susan said. "A balcony from which we can see the ocean. Sun flooding down on us."

Heimrich said, "Mmmm," with doubt in the sound, and went out of the cabin and, by elevator, up to the wireless room.

There was a different operator on duty. He also had been instructed. Heimrich gave him the London number he had called before, and the operator said, "Sì, signor. Charged to the ship. I shall ring in Booth One when we are through."

Heimrich opened the door of Booth One and sat down beside it and waited for the bell to ring. It was longer this time. It was two cigarettes longer. Sir Ronald probably had been wise to give up cigarettes. Although in the end it had done him no good to give up cigarettes. If he had enjoyed smoking, he might as well have kept on with it.

The bell rang in the booth.

He got the number repeated in crisp tone. He said, "Continental Forwarding?" and got a "Certainly, sir. Can I help you?"

"Mr. Parsons, please."

"Who shall I say is calling?"

The old routine; the weary routine. Heimrich told the girl who she should say was calling. Then the routine changed. The girl said, "Inspector Heimrich? Mr. Parsons has been expecting you to call. One moment, please."

The next voice was male and light and quick.

"Parsons here. You're Police Inspector Heimrich? Of Troop K, New York State Police?"

"Yes."

"May I have your badge number, Inspector?"

So. It had seemed to Continental Forwarding, Limited, worth the trouble of checking on. Which was interesting. Which possibly accounted for Parson's delay in calling. Heimrich gave him the badge number.

There was a momentary delay. Then Parsons said, "Checks out. You called to ask if Sir Ronald Grimes had telephoned this office. Were told we were closed for the day. Right?"

"Quite right, Mr. Parsons."

"Little confusion about that," Parsons said. "Hadn't been informed, Miss Brightly hadn't. He did call. I talked to him myself, matter of fact. Routine matter."

"Mr. Parsons," Heimrich said, "Sir Ronald has disappeared from the ship. Apparently he has gone overboard. This call to you was the last call he made, so far as I can find out. We check on such things when we're policemen. As you, apparently, have checked out on me."

"Matter of routine," Parsons said.

"This routine matter? That Sir Ronald called you about? From mid-ocean. At considerable expense."

"Some things he had in Washington," Parsons said. "Furniture. Things like that. Wanted them here in England. We are handling that. Were, anyway. He called to ask if things were moving along. See what I mean?"

"No. I can't say I do. He thought—oh, that some difficulty had come up?"

"You can put it that way, yes."

161

"In mid-ocean," Heimrich said, "he suddenly starts to worry about his furniture and things like that. Calls up at what, by your time, would be late evening. Were you able to reassure him, Mr. Parsons?"

"Absolutely. Everything in train, y'know."

"Continental Forwarding. Just what do you forward, Mr. Parsons?"

"Quite a few things. Variety of things, you might call it."

"Sir Ronald wasn't having you ship his furniture, or whatever, to Yugoslavia, by any chance? To—or say in care of—A. Schmidt Gesellschaft in Zagreb?"

There was a long pause. Then Parsons said, in a voice deeper, and harder, than it had been before. "A Schmidt Gesellschaft, you say. How'd you come by that, Inspector?"

"Sir Ronald," Heimrich said, "had jotted the name down. With an address, or what I take to be an address." He read from the penciled lines on the inside of the match folder what he took to be an address.

"Sir Ronald had?"

"I can't be sure he had. Lady Grimes doubts it was his handwriting. Somebody did. On the inside of a match folder. May just have dropped the folder, of course. Somebody else I mean, naturally. And Sir Ronald may have absently picked it up and put it in his pocket. Only, Lady Grimes says he'd given up smoking."

Parsons did not say anything.

"I take it," Heimrich said, "that you're familiar with A. Schmidt Gesellschaft. Have had dealings with them, perhaps? Forwarded things to them?"

Parsons laughed, as if Heimrich had said something funny. Heimrich waited.

"Dealings," Parsons said. "No, I shouldn't call it that, precisely, Inspector. Say—" He paused again, as a man does who wants to pick his words with care. "You might say we're competing firms, Inspector. Yes, I think it might be put that way."

"In this forwarding business? Whatever that may be."

"Way of putting it. Yes."

"As a front for what, Mr. Parsons? As a cover for what?"

"Afraid I don't know what you mean," Parsons said. And he spoke, Heimrich thought, in the tone of one who understands perfectly well what is meant.

"You're not being helpful," Heimrich said. "A man in the British diplomatic service has fallen overboard. Or been pushed overboard. A detective inspector of the London police has been strangled. You're not being helpful, Mr. Parsons. I take it you don't want to be."

"I'm sorry, Inspector. I've told you all I can. All I'm allowed—" He did not finish.

"Which is nothing."

"We do know about this A. Schmidt concern. Have for a considerable time. All I can tell you, I'm afraid."

"Which is no help."

"Sorry about that. Rules, you know. Lady Grimes? She's making do?"

"Barely. With difficulty."

"Plans to leave the ship at Lisbon, I understand," Parsons said. "Right?"

"I believe so. You want to get in touch with her about this —furniture you're shipping for her? For her husband at first. Now for her?"

"A way of putting it."

"How did you learn she plans to leave the ship at Lisbon?"

There was, again, a pause.

"Say we're just guessing," Parsons said. "Likely thing for her to do, wouldn't you say? Want to be with your own people at such a time, I'd think. Just—call it a supposition on our part."

"She hasn't called you from the ship? Called Continental Forwarding, Limited? There'll be a record if she has, you know."

163

"No. Why would she do that?"

"To tell you she's leaving the ship at Lisbon," Heimrich said. "Not going to Trieste, as they originally planned to do."

"No. Lady Grimes did not call us. Anything else?"

"Nothing you will give me," Heimrich said, and put the receiver back on its hook.

Stone walls everywhere, Heimrich thought. He wondered if Sir Robert Mason at the British Embassy in Washington would be more enlightening about A. Schmidt Gesellschaft and thought briefly about calling to find out. He looked at his watch. Elven in the morning. Much earlier in the morning in Washington. Hardly light there yet.

And not much here, Merton Heimrich thought, and went back to Cabin 82. Susan was not there. He used the telephone. Louis Cataldi was still unconscious. The security men had not found any fellow steward to whom Louis had mentioned any experience of his during his Wednesday-Thursday tour of duty.

He might, Heimrich thought, go up to the promenade deck and have a cup of consommé with Susan. He might—

The telephone rang.

He picked it up quickly. Louis might have recovered consciousness. He might—

"Heimrich."

"Ellen Grimes here. That match folder you asked about, Inspector. I've—I've been trying to remember. There was something about a match folder I remember. Think I remember. It's probably nothing that will help. But—but I want to help, Inspector."

Heimrich said, "Yes, Lady Grimes?"

"Do you want to come to my cabin and—no, they're just coming to make it up. On the promenade deck? Our—" Her voice faded for a moment. One uses the plural when it isn't right any more, as one uses the present tense, the mind rebelling against the past tense. "My deck chair is on the starboard side. About amidships, I think. If you?"

"Yes, Lady Grimes. I'll be along."

He climbed stairs to the promenade deck. He went through one of the forward doors and walked aft. Susan was in her chair, with a cup of consommé in her hand. But she was not alone. Mrs. Lucinda Powers was sitting beside her, in Merton Heimrich's chair. She was leaning toward Susan, and she was talking—talking in what was apparently a monologue. Susan saw Heimrich and lifted her cup slightly to show she saw him. But she just perceptibly shook her head. Lucinda Powers was, apparently, being worth listening to. Heimrich went on along the deck; went half a dozen deck-chair lengths along it. Ellen Grimes was tucking a folded blanket back of her head in an outboard chair. He sat down in the chair beside hers. He held a pack of cigarettes out to her, and she took one. He was reaching for his lighter when she took a lighter out of a handbag on the deck beside her and flicked it. No fire appeared. She flicked it again, and there was a spark, but again no fire. She said, "Damn the thing. Half the time—" and leaned toward Merton Heimrich, who had his lighter out. It worked. She said, "Kew." Then she said, "Ronald kept it working for me. Flints and things. Whatever they need. But still it's only a part-time lighter. Which is what made me begin to remember."

He waited.

"It was at the club in Washington," she said. "About the match folder. That's what I'm getting around to. Trying to remember."

He said, "Yes, Lady Grimes."

"We were having dinner at the club," she said. "We did sometimes. About two weeks ago. Oh, perhaps ten days ago. Two or three days before we sailed. Only then we were going to fly BOAC. Going by ship was—oh, a last-minute decision. If—if we'd only flown as we planned. If only—"

He waited. Then, after rather a long pause, during which

165

she turned away from him and looked out at the ocean, she said, "Where was I, Inspector? Things—things keep coming in."

"Yes," he said. "You were having dinner at the club. The Field and Tennis Club, that would have been?"

"Yes. We were having cocktails in the lounge before we went in to have dinner. There were a good many people in the lounge. A good many people go to the club for dinner on Fridays. That's it. It was the Friday before we sailed. They have seafood on Fridays. Prawns. Lobsters. Things like that. I'm wandering, aren't I? Things—things don't seem to come straight just now. We were having drinks. The two of us—the, the two of us. At a table meant for four. There was a table we liked better, but we were too late to get it. This one was off at a side, near the telephone booths. There are three booths in the lounge. People are all the time getting calls there. Important people getting important calls, I expect. Inspector, I'm sorry. I can't seem to go in a straight line."

He said, "You're doing fine, Lady Grimes," although she certainly was not. "You were at this table for four. Having cocktails before dinner."

"Ian Whitney came in," she said. "He was wearing a dinner jacket, so I thought he must be going on somewhere, because people don't dress at the club much. It's an informal sort of place most nights. Which was one of the reasons Ronald liked —" Again she broke off and looked at the ocean. She said, "I'm sorry, Inspector. I can't help it."

She was still in shock, Heimrich thought. She was coming out of it. Her face was not as dragged down as it had been. But she was still in shock.

"Major Whitney came in," he said. "You're doing fine, Lady Grimes."

"I'll try to be clearer," she said, and turned in her chair to face him. "Ian Whitney came in and—"

Whitney had stopped just inside the door of the lounge

166

and looked around it, as one does seeking a vacant table. Then he had seen the Grimeses and saluted them across the room, and then walked across it to their table. He had said, "Mind?" and when neither minded, had pulled out a chair and sat at the table. He had waved his hand toward a waiter.

"They're colored waiters at the club," Ellen Grimes said. "Ian called them all 'Joe.' I don't know that they liked that too much. Or, sometimes, just 'Boy.' Ronald never did that. They're all nice people. Ronald knew all their names."

Again she paused. This time the pause was more brief.

The waiter had come, and Major Ian Whitney had said, "Whisky and water, boy. No ice," and the man had said, "Yes, sir, Major," and gone off. Ian Whitney had hoped they didn't mind his barging in; had said he had only time for a quick one because he was "due at a do." The "quick one" came quickly. Whitney drank quickly from the glass. Then he looked around the room.

"As if he were looking for someone," Ellen Grimes said. "But I don't know whether I thought that at the time. It's the way it seems to me now. That he was—oh, expectant. He said, 'Been a fine day,' or something like that. He asked whether we had got in any tennis. We hadn't. We'd spent most of the day packing to—to go home. We had reservations for a Sunday morning flight. Then—"

Whitney kept looking around the room. He saw a few people he knew and nodded to them. "Or saluted them. He is likely to salute people. Of course, he's army." He still, to Ellen Grimes, seemed to be waiting for somebody. Or for something.

"I feel now that I felt that way. I'm not sure I did then."

Whitney was halfway through his drink; Ronald Grimes had signaled a waiter for another round. "He was drinking sherry. He did, mostly. Sometimes whisky but mostly, before dinner, a glass or two of sherry."

The waiter came, and Sir Ronald said, "Same again, Wil-

167

liam," and the waiter said, "Sir Ronald," and went away. But then another waiter came. He said, "Major Whitney, sir. A telephone call for you, sir. In the Number Two booth."

Whitney pushed back his chair. He said, "Probably wonder where I've got to," and went to the booth. He went into it and closed the door.

"We could see him through the glass," Ellen Grimes said. "The way we were sitting, Ronald could see him better than I could. I could just make out that he seemed to be writing something down. It was only for a minute, anyway."

Whitney came back from the telephone booth and said, "Supposed to be at this do, y'know." But he sat down and lifted his glass again.

"Probably want a cigarette, don't you, Ellen?" Ronald Grimes said.

("I hadn't been thinking about a cigarette particularly. But there was something in the way he said it.")

There had been more than that. Grimes had taken a pack of cigarettes out of his pocket and held it out.

("He carried them for me sometimes. Particularly in the evening, when I had an evening purse.")

She took a cigarette and got her lighter out of the purse on her lap. "This lighter." She flicked it, and it did not light. Ronald Grimes fingered in his pocket for matches. "Sometimes he carried them for me, too. But not always. Not this time. It's coming back clearly now."

"You're doing fine, Lady Grimes," Heimrich said.

"You asked me about a match folder," she said. "The one you have with something written in it. Then I remembered about this. But I'm probably just taking up your time, aren't I?"

"I don't know," Heimrich said. "Go on, Lady Grimes."

Ronald Grimes had taken the lighter from his wife's fingers, but it had not worked for him either. "Almost always he could make it work."

"Happen to have a match on you, Whitney?" Ronald

Grimes asked and, after a second of hesitation—"The way I remember it now, Inspector"—Whitney had taken a folder of club matches from a pocket of his dinner jacket. He started to open it. But Grimes held out a hand for the matches and Whitney gave the folder to him.

Ronald Grimes broke a match out of the folder and lighted his wife's cigarette. Then he put the folder in his pocket.

"Sorry, old man," Ian Whitney said and held his hand out. "Need them at this do. Never have any around, y'know."

Sir Ronald Grimes said, "Sorry," in his turn, and took a match folder out of his pocket and held it out to Whitney. Whitney put it in his pocket and finished his drink and said, "Got to trot along to this do." He beckoned a waiter and signed his drink check. He went along, not exactly trotting but not strolling either.

"And that's all," Ellen Grimes said. "I thought it might mean something to you. Now it just seems—entirely trivial."

"When he wanted to light your cigarette," Heimrich said. "After the lighter wouldn't work, Sir Ronald reached in a pocket. You thought for matches. And didn't find any?"

"I thought that."

"The jacket pocket? Right hand? He was right-handed?"

"Yes. Oh, yes. He always carries—he always carried things in the right-hand pocket. Little things, I mean. The cigarettes he was carrying for me. Matches, when he remembered."

"Dropped Whitney's matches into that pocket?"

"I expect so. I don't really remember."

"Gave Whitney back the same folder of matches?"

"Club matches," Ellen Grimes said. "With the name of the club on the folder and a little squiggle. Meant to look like a coat of arms, or something. Yes. I suppose it was the same folder. They're all alike."

"When your husband lighted your cigarette," Heimrich said. "Happen to notice whether there were many matches left in it?"

"No, Inspector."

169

"Or whether anything was written on the inside of the flap?"

She shook her head.

"You think now this—" He took the folder out of his pocket and held it open for her—"this isn't your husband's writing?"

She took the folder from him and looked at it for some seconds. She handed it back. She said, "I'm almost sure it isn't. Of course, there's not much to go on, is there?"

"No," Heimrich said. "You happen to know how Major Whitney writes? What his writing looks like?"

She did not. She did not think she had ever seen anything Whitney had written. She was quite sure she had not. "We don't—we didn't, I mean—know Ian at all well. He wouldn't have written to us."

"But your husband might have? Known Major Whitney's handwriting, I mean?"

"I don't know."

"At the office," Heimrich said. "Handwritten memos. That sort of thing?"

"Perhaps. I don't know, Inspector. Does what I've been telling you mean anything?"

"I don't know, Lady Grimes. When did you and Sir Ronald decide to go home by ship? Instead of by air? After this incident at the club?"

"The next day, I think. Ronald said something like, 'Let's take it easy. Go round by Venice.' Something like that. I was glad. I don't really like to fly. You're—oh, so sealed in. You think, Suppose something happened and we had to get out. And think you couldn't ever get out."

"Your husband didn't have trouble getting cabins in the ship so late on?"

"I don't know. Probably he had to pull strings. He could when he had to."

⚒ 13

Heimrich thanked Ellen Grimes and left her sitting in her chair, looking out at the quiet ocean. He walked forward slowly toward his own chair, and toward Susan.

It had taken Lady Grimes some hours to remember about the match folder. It might not, of course, have been an incident of any special significance to her—might have been an entirely trivial matter which would slip from the memory until a match folder with writing in it brought it back to memory. The same match folder? There was no assurance of that. He was supposed to think so. He was supposed to think that Major Ian Whitney, not Sir Ronald Grimes, had noted down an address in a match folder; had noted it down on what was convenient when he was given it on the telephone.

Taken her hours to remember. Or, of course, to invent. If invented, then because "A. Schmidt Gesellschaft" was an address with some special meaning. An address, knowledge of which would be incriminating? A cover address? An address, apparently, known to a man named Parsons, managing director of a firm called Continental Forwarding, Limited. Another cover outfit, Heimrich thought. And one to which Sir Ronald

Grimes had talked on the evening before his disappearance. Almost certainly, now, before his death. Engaged in the same operations, Continental Forwarding, Limited, and A. Schmidt Gesellschaft? Parsons had said "competing" firms. On the opposite sides of a fence, then? Or, of a curtain? Parsons had made, or had somebody make, a transatlantic call to check the bona fides of a man who said he was Inspector M. L. Heimrich, New York State Police.

He had got the confirmation he wanted. There is nothing especially secret about the badge numbers of policemen. Still, some reason would have to have been given. There would have had to be more than, "This is Continental Forwarding, Limited. What is the badge number of an Inspector M. L. Heimrich?" The answer to so bare a question would have been, "Why do you want to know?" or "What business is it of yours, Continental Forwarding, Limited?" Somebody in the New York State Police must have been told what business it was of Continental Forwarding. And must have been convinced.

Heimrich's deck chair was empty now. He sat down in it and felt he sat heavily. Like a—

Susan smiled and shook her head. In addition to everything else, Merton thought, she reads minds.

"Mrs. Powers seemed to be talking a blue streak," he said.

She nodded her head. "Very blue," she said. "Very streaky. About her late husband, and how Sir Ronald did him in. In some fashion she still doesn't make clear. And what a dreadful man Sir Ronald was, although he fooled some people. And about that wife of his, who makes people think she's so innocent. 'Butter wouldn't melt in her mouth.' She actually said that, Merton. I didn't know people ever did. And that the British government should have kept an eye on Sir Ronald."

"Why?"

"She didn't say. She—she just talks. On and on. Never very clearly. Hints and half hints. But she really hated Ronald Grimes, Merton. That's clear enough."

172

"Why tell all this to you?"

"I'd think because I'm Mrs. M. L. Heimrich, dear. Wouldn't you? And might pass on the word that Sir Ronald was a no-good so-and-so and better over the rail than not."

"It's upside down," Merton Heimrich said. "Not that everything isn't at the moment. But if a man's been killed, you don't make a point of how much you hated him. That sort of thing can give people ideas."

"Does it, dear?"

"Nothing seems to this morning. Possibilities." He looked beyond Susan at the quiet ocean. "Of which I have too many."

"She looks like a strong woman," Susan said. "She moves well. These chairs aren't all that easy to get out of. She—oh, swirled out. Said, 'I've bored you long enough, Mrs. Heimrich,' and then, well, just wasn't there any more. Not that it wasn't a relief. You're tired, aren't you? By Lady Grimes?"

"Her. A man named Parsons in London. A man named Mason in Washington. Something called A. Schmidt Gesellschaft, probably in Zagreb. By Major Ian Whitney, in the *Italia*. Unless he's fallen overboard too."

"He hasn't. At least ten minutes or so ago he hadn't. He was sitting in a deck chair, facing outboard. He was watching you and Lady Grimes, I think. After Mrs. Powers let me off the hook I looked around—looked aft—to see where you'd gone. And saw. And saw Major Whitney too."

"Yes," Heimrich said. "I saw him too."

"Is it too early for Mario?" Susan said.

He looked at his watch. It was a quarter of twelve.

"A little," he said. "Anyway, there's a call I ought to make. Something I forgot."

She said, "Oh," her voice diminished.

"Not a long one," he told her. "Nor far away. I'll come back and we'll go see Mario."

He swung out of the chair.

(He moves so well, she thought. With so little effort for so

173

big a man. There's nothing puzzled about the way he moves.)

Heimrich found a telephone. He got the purser's office, and then got the chief steward. He verified the security men's findings—if Louis Cataldi had had anything unusual happen to him Wednesday night, he had not told any of his fellow stewards about it. Or none of them remembered that he had.

"His belongings?"

"In his locker, signor. Clothes. A picture of a man with mustachios. Very large mustachios. His father, it is possible, signor."

"Money?"

"Two five-hundred-lira notes, signor. A few American coins. A dollar bill. Not money."

Heimrich called the ship's hospital. Louis was still unconscious. He had, however, said a few words. They had not seemed to mean anything. They had been more sounds than words. Money? In the clothing he had been wearing when he was hit? No, signor. Oh, a dollar bill. Perhaps two dollar bills.

If Louis had seen something and had tried to collect on what he had seen, he hadn't collected. Except, of course, a blow on the head. Delivered by whom? And with what?

Heimrich went back to the promenade deck. Susan was watching for him. He nodded his head and beckoned. She was out of her chair and walking toward him.

(She moves with springs. I lumber.)

They went to see Mario in the *veranda belvedere*. The four Frenchmen were already there. They were smoking their cigars. There were few others in Mario's bar. Mario beamed at them. The four Frenchmen blew smoke into the air.

Susan dislikes cigar smoke. The dislike of cigar smoke is almost an obsession with her.

"We're almost the first," she said, as Mario went to get their drinks. "We drink more on holiday, don't we?"

"To prove it's a holiday," Merton Heimrich said, his voice low and with a depressed note in it. "The only proof we've got, and I'm sorry."

174

She smiled at him and patted his hand for an instant. She said, "It's funny all that cigar smoke doesn't bother me the way it usually does."

"Air conditioning," Heimrich told her. "Whole ship is. Thank you, Mario."

They sipped. They had half finished their drink when a steward came in and said something to Mario. Mario nodded his head, and nodded it toward the Heimrichs. The steward came to their table. He said, "Signor Heimrich? *Telegramma*, Signor Heimrich."

Heimrich said, "Thanks," and provided a quarter and got "*Grazie*, signor." He opened the wireless message. It was brief:

"Permitted tell Schmidt East German agency. Parsons."

A stone in the wall loosened? Or one set in place?

Heimrich read the message again, this time aloud.

"It means something?" Susan said.

"Earlier you said something about spies," Heimrich said. "Joking, we both thought. Maybe you weren't, dear. Even if you thought you were. Parsons is something called 'Continental Forwarding, Limited.' Very close-mouthed, until now. Got permission from somebody to open up a little."

He put the message in a jacket pocket. She looked at him and raised her eyebrows.

"The match folder," he said. "I told you about it. Or meant to, anyway."

She shook her head. He told her about it, briefly. He told her where he had found it and of Ellen Grimes's suggested explanation. She said, "The major?"

"According to her story," Heimrich said. "Which she took a time to remember. Or, to think up, naturally. She—"

He stopped abruptly. He raised his glass and held it toward hers and, slowly, she met his glass with hers. "To the Costa del Sol," Heimrich said, and she raised her shoulders slightly and repeated his words. Then she looked around the room, into which people had begun to trickle.

One of those who had come in was Major Ian Whitney. He did not trickle in. He walked in erect and resolute, and Mario met him and said, "Signor Major. One, signor?"

Whitney said, "Minute, what?" and instead of following Mario came to the Heimrichs' table.

"Morning, Inspector. Mrs. Heimrich," Whitney said. "Wonder if you can spare me a few minutes, Inspector? Something I may be able to clear up for you."

"Glad to have things cleared up," Heimrich said. "Now?"

"No hurry," Whitney said. "After lunch. My cabin be all right? Two-thirtyish be all right?"

"Yes," Heimrich said, and Whitney walked—or marched— to the table Mario stood by.

"The wireless message?" Susan said. Heimrich shrugged his shoulders. "They could have paged you in the main cocktail lounge," Susan said. "Gone around saying, 'Inspector Heimrich, please. *Telegramma*, please.' "

"Yes," Heimrich said. "Or he may have seen the man come in with the *telegramma*. Also, he wasn't sitting too far away when I was talking to Lady Grimes."

"Close enough to watch," Susan said. "To hear—overhear —I shouldn't think so. Unless he has very good ears. You'll have a chance to ask him, apparently."

Heimrich said, "Yes." He looked at their almost-empty glasses and then at Susan.

"Yes," she said. "To prove it's a holiday. And to the Costa del Sol."

Mario had also seen the almost-empty glasses. Mario was everywhere and saw everything. He came to their table and said, "Sir? Madam?"

"Yes."

"It is calm today," Mario said. "The sea is behaving herself, signor."

Heimrich said, "Yes," again and, as before, he seemed to be speaking from a long way off.

Mario carried away their empty glasses and brought back

176

filled glasses. He also brought a dish of nuts. Susan said, "Thank you, Mario." Merton said nothing at all, which was unlike him. They sipped from their glasses and said little, and after a time the lunch chimes sounded. The four Frenchmen led the way, their cigars still alight.

There was no partly filled wine bottle on their table. They had finished the last of a bottle the night before. Their waiter said, "The wine steward, signor?" but Heimrich did not appear to hear him, and Susan smiled at the waiter and shook her head. There isn't much point in trying to prove it's a holiday, Susan thought. And it worries him so. But now, I think, it isn't that which is worrying him. He's submerged, now. Which means—which I hope means—that it's nearly over.

They finished lunch. "A while on the deck for me," Susan said. "Then a nap, I think."

"I'm sorry," Heimrich said. "I'm sorry as hell, darling."

She laughed lightly. Then she said, "Shhh, my dear."

"I'll find you," he said, and she smiled up at him and said, "Always, Merton."

He went up to the sun deck and the wireless station, with which he was getting wearily familiar. After rather a long wait, he got the British Embassy in Washington—and more static than ever.

Sir Robert Mason was gone for the weekend.

He looked at his watch. It was two-fifteen. But "-ish" provides latitude. He went the two flights down to the boat deck and turned left toward the starboard corridor. Directly ahead of him, beyond a wide passageway and an elevator, was a door to the open promenade—a passageway and door that anyone going straight from the *veranda belvedere* to the starboard cabins—Cabin 16, say—would have to pass. It was from here, probably, that Sir Ronald had been decoyed—or more likely knocked unconscious and carried or dragged—to the rail over which he was heaved. Probably as soon as he and Hunt had left the lounge and separated, Hunt to go below to his own quarters.

177

Heimrich went aft to Cabin 10. The door was closed. He pressed the buzzer button and after some seconds heard, "Come in," and went in.

Whitney was sitting on his bed and was fitting a tennis racket into its case, which seemed to Heimrich an odd thing to be doing in mid ocean. He saw enough of the racket before it disappeared into its case to see that it had a steel frame.

"Meeting friends in Lisbon," Whitney said. "Going to their club with them, y'know. Great one for tennis. Get in a set or two, perhaps." He tossed the cased tennis racket onto the bed. "Checking on the stringing while I waited for you," Whitney said. "Damp sea air's hard on gut, y'know."

Heimrich said he supposed so.

"Didn't get you here to talk about tennis," Whitney said. "Have them bring us in a drink, what?"

"No," Heimrich said. "Had a couple before lunch. What did you want to see me about, Major?"

"Right," Whitney said. "Get down to it. Saw you talking to Lady Grimes this morning, didn't I? Showed her something. Looked like a match folder from the club. That right, Inspector?"

"You've good eyes, Major."

"Something written inside the folder, way I saw it. Gave it to her, and she read it. That right?"

"There was something written inside the folder. Yes, Major?"

"At a guess," Whitney said, "it was an address. An address —say on the other side of the Iron Curtain?"

"It's your guess, Major."

Major Whitney nodded his head, apparently in approval. He said, "Cagy, aren't you? Found this match folder in Grimes's cabin, I shouldn't wonder? Must have hidden it there, wouldn't you say? Grimes himself, I mean."

"It wasn't too much hidden."

"Silly ass not to have merely remembered the address.

Torn the folder up. Hell, burned it up. Where'd you find it, Inspector? Not just lying around on a table or something. I'd wager on that."

"No."

"You showed it to Lady Grimes," Whitney said. "She— how'd she take it? Seem surprised? That sort of thing?"

"She didn't think it was her husband's writing."

"I'll wager she didn't," Whitney said. "Hundred quid to tuppence she didn't. Say whose she thought it was? Or do you want me to guess, Inspector?"

"If you want to."

"Not difficult. I'd a notion they'd rumbled me. And Hunt too. Wily pair, the Grimeses are. She's wily for both now, of course. Probably leave the ship at Lisbon and fly on to London. Innocent as a lamb, what?"

"Innocent of what, Major?"

"You mean you haven't figured it out?" He shook his head. "Puts me in a bit of a spot," he said. "No ill of the dead. Sort of thing we don't like to spread around, y'know. Fine old family, the Grimeses. Goes back centuries. Manor house and that sort of thing. And—well, to break with all that. Damn strange. I'll say that. Rough on his son, y'know. Have to resign his commission, I shouldn't wonder. When it comes out. As it's bound to now, y'know. No way of covering it up. That was the idea, y'know. Some of our people meet him at Lisbon and—just ease him home. No fuss. Nothing in the press. Can't handle it that way now, thanks to you, Inspector."

"To me?"

"Oh, in a way of speaking. Realized you were aboard and —call it panicked. Went over the side on his own, rather than face up to it. Comes to that, wouldn't you say?"

Heimrich shook his head. He was the picture of a sorely puzzled man. He said, "You'll have to be clearer, Major. You're talking in circles. Want to go back a ways? You wanted to guess whose writing Lady Grimes thought it might be in the match folder. You didn't guess. You want to now? To clear things up a bit?"

"Oh," Whitney said, "probably mine. Attack the best defense and that sort of thing. Something about my joining them for cocktails at the club, what? And—I don't know the details she made up. Telephone call for me, perhaps? And I went into the booth and wrote something down on the inside of a match folder? And—" He shrugged. "Grimes switched the folders? Something like that?"

"It's your guess, Major. Go on guessing."

"I can't fill it in, y'know. Don't know how her mind would work, actually. But she's a wily person, as I said. And in on it up to her neck. Too bad. Rather a pretty neck. But there it is."

"All right. Where is what?"

Heimrich let impatience sound in his voice.

"Not onto it yet? Sir Ronald Grimes, Bart, was going over to the other side. We'd—got onto him. Hunt was sent to the States to take a hand. What the Special Branch is for, among other things. Hunt and I—well, we worked together. And got what we needed. He'd been passing things along, y'know. Top secret things. Not the first time it's happened at the Embassy. Give you that. Sir Robert—Robert Mason that is—rumbled it first. Reason I was assigned to Washington. Reason they sent Hunt over. We—well, say we got the goods on him. And he found out we had. So—time to get moving, he figured. Must have been a bit of a shock to them when Hunt and I turned up aboard this ship. So, he had to do Hunt in. Or thought he had to. Hunt had plenty in that briefcase of his. Get it, even if it meant killing Hunt. Throw it over the side."

"And then kill himself, Major? I take it you are a major?"

"Oh, yes. With—call it a sideline, shall we? What you Yanks call a troubleshooter?"

Heimrich said, "Mmmm." Then he said, "This story Lady Grimes told me. About your having written an address down in a match folder. Not the way it was, I gather?"

"We were having cocktails at this club," Whitney sa... "That's the way she probably told you. And it's true. To a point it's true. Then Grimes got this telephone call and went into a booth to take it. And wrote Schmidt's address down on a match folder. I could see him writing through the glass of the booth. And could guess what he was getting. The address of the contact he was to make in Zagreb. On his way—well, on his way elsewhere, if you know what I mean. Any of the Iron Curtain countries. The boss country, probably. Happen to have that match folder with you, Inspector? Might be useful to us, y'know."

"No, Major. Not on me. In my cabin. You saw Sir Ronald writing something down? This address, you assume?"

"Had to be that way. From a contact in Washington."

"Wrote it down and kept the folder. In his pocket. As you said, rather a silly thing to do. Sort of thing you'd commit to memory, I'd think."

"I would in his place, certainly. But—they slip up, don't they? You must know that, Inspector."

"Yes," Heimrich said, "they slip up, Major. Helpful to us when they do."

Merton Heimrich stood up and looked down at Major Whitney.

"How did you know the address was of somebody named Schmidt?" Heimrich said. "In Zagreb? He show you the address in the folder? When he already knew you had, as you put it, rumbled him? Or—how *did* you know? If you weren't told it yourself, and didn't write it down yourself? If it wasn't the way that Lady Grimes told me it was?"

"Schmidt? I didn't say anything—"

And then his face changed, as he remembered.

He could have wriggled out of it, Heimrich thought. He could have said that A. Schmidt Gesellschaft was a cover long since blown to other people in his "sideline." As it had been, obviously, to a man named Parsons, who was clearly in the line of business Whitney claimed he was in. Whitney hadn't

181

seen the place to wriggle through. He wasn't as wily—

He stopped thinking because Whitney was getting up. He was getting up with the cased tennis racket in his hand—the steel-framed tennis racket. Then he had the case off the racket, and his strong hands were quick.

They were not quick enough. Heimrich was on holiday and had no gun. But he had hands and they, too, were strong and quick. He hit Whitney on the jaw as Whitney, on his feet, pulled the uncased racket back and high in his right hand, held sidewise so that the steel edge would crack down on Heimrich's head.

Whitney fell back on the bed, and the tennis racket fell to the deck. Whitney wasn't out—not, anyway, too much out to listen.

Heimrich picked the racket up and looked at it.

"Strings seem to be all right," Heimrich said, in a conversational tone. "Damp sea air doesn't seem to have damaged it. But then, the ship's air-conditioned, isn't it, Whitney? Dehumidified. So it wasn't the gut you were worried about, was it? Trying to make sure there wasn't any blood in the groove the gut fits into. From the last time you used it. Not on a tennis court, Whitney. On the deck outside. To hit a man—a boy, really—who had seen you come out of Hunt's cabin the night Hunt was strangled. And—tried to shake you down, Whitney? It was that way, wasn't it?"

I'm wasting my breath, Heimrich thought. The man's out. And he won't get to Trieste on his way to A. Schmidt Gellschaft in Zagreb. Or, as he said himself, "elsewhere."

Heimrich picked up the telephone.

⚘ 14

It was late afternoon when Heimrich went the now familiar way to the quarters of Comandante Antonio di Scarlotti. Major Ian Whitney was in what the young officer in charge of two security men chose to call "detention quarters." Merton Heimrich had talked to Louis Cataldi, whose speech was rather blurred, and whose head ached, and who spoke in Italian and had to be translated out of it. Heimrich had sent two wireless messages, one to Continental Forwarding, Limited, attention "Parsons," and the other to Sir Robert Mason, British Embassy, Washington. Mason was evidently on a long weekend and might not get the message for hours, or even for days. Heimrich doubted whether Parsons took long weekends.

Both messages were the same:

"Whitney killed Grimes and Hunt. But evidence insufficient. Heimrich."

He took along a copy of the message to break the news to Comandante di Scarlotti, who wouldn't, Heimrich supposed, be pleased. He had already had one answer, and took that along too. It read:

183

"Our dirty linen. Meeting ship Lisbon. Parsons."

Di Scarlotti was drinking coffee. He had coffee brought for Heimrich. He said, "We are in your debt, Inspector. Greatly in your debt. The line is in your debt and the authorities of my nation."

He spoke as if he had had the words ready—and a little as if he were awarding a medal.

Heimrich sipped coffee and lighted the cigarette di Scarlotti had offered him and then, slowly, he shook his head. He said, "Better read this, Captain," and gave di Scarlotti the copy of the message he had sent to Parsons and Sir Robert Mason. Di Scarlotti read it twice. He looked at Heimrich.

"I do not understand," he said. " 'Evidence insufficient.' Why do you say that, Inspector?"

"Because it's true," Heimrich said. "Yes, I'm quite certain Whitney pushed, or threw, Sir Ronald overboard. Probably knocked him out first. That he strangled Hunt. That he killed them both because they could have stopped his defecting. They had documentary evidence. That he had been leaking information—secret information—from the British Embassy ιo agents of—let's say foreign powers. Whether for money or from conviction I don't know. Earlier, he'd been assigned the other side of the Curtain. And was ritually kicked out. Which may have been a device, a cover. How he was persuaded we'll never know, because he isn't going to talk to us. Oh, he'll talk. Tell his own story—that Sir Ronald was giving information to the other side; that he, Whitney, was an intelligence officer who planned to expose Grimes. That Hunt had been working with him in Washington, not with Sir Ronald. And, Captain, we can't prove he's lying."

"He killed two men in my ship," di Scarlotti said. "You do not seem to understand, Inspector. This is an Italian ship. She is covered by Italian law. Murder aboard her—Inspector, it is a matter for the Italian authorities. You do not seem to understand."

184

Heimrich drew deeply on his cigarette and crushed it out. He drank from his cup.

"I said I was certain, Captain," Heimrich said. "I'm sure Whitney knocked Sir Ronald out, probably with the steel-framed tennis racket, and then lifted him over the rail and let go of him. And that he then went down to Hunt's cabin and strangled him. To get his briefcase and the documents in it. And to shut his mouth, of course. He must have thought that that—well, as we say, that that would get him off the hook. I don't think it would have. I think Sir Ronald had already been in touch with a man named Parsons who is—oh, I suppose counterespionage, if that's what the English call it. As Grimes himself probably was. But Whitney didn't know that. Or, if he suspected it, thought he could bluff it out with the documents, whatever they were, destroyed. And two voices silenced.

"There was another voice he had to try to silence—and in a way he has. This young steward of yours—"

"This former steward," di Scarlotti said. "I assure you, Inspector. Former."

"Cataldi," Heimrich said. "Saw Whitney come out of Hunt's cabin and recognized him and tried blackmail. Which, understandably, Cataldi's not going to admit. Whitney tried to kill him with this racket of his and couldn't finish the job because I happened to interrupt him. Yes. I am quite sure of these things. Can I prove them? No."

"I do not understand. Are you saying—but surely you are not saying—that he is to escape justice? As you would say, 'get away with murder'?"

"Nobody saw him throw Sir Ronald overboard," Heimrich said. "He did go to Hunt's cabin Wednesday night. At any rate, young Louis saw a man come out of it sometime before midnight. But—Louis won't say who. And Whitney will deny he was there. Or say he had gone to see Hunt to talk about— oh, about their next step in stopping Sir Ronald's plan to de-

185

fect. That Hunt was alive when he left. We can't prove he wasn't, you know."

"You say Louis tried to blackmail him. And that he attacked Louis. Inspector, you saw that happen yourself."

"No," Heimrich said. "I heard a sound. I saw a shadow running. I can't identify the shadow. I found Louis Cataldi with a bad head wound. And—Louis says only that the man he saw was one of the passengers. He cannot identify the man. A tall man, he thinks. He did not see whether the man was carrying an attaché case. He says. He did not hear until late Thursday afternoon that a man—a Signor Hunt—had been murdered. He did wonder whether the man he saw leaving Hunt's cabin was the man who killed him. Yes, he wondered that. But he could not identify the man. Anyway, it was not his business."

Di Scarlotti said something in Italian. What he said was brief and spoken in an angry voice, and Heimrich suspected it was a terse description of one Louis Cataldi.

"He did not try to blackmail Major Whitney. How could he when he did not know the man was Major Whitney? He was not hit by anyone. He had gone to the boat deck—the open promenade—to get some air before he went on duty. He slipped. Stumbled. Fell against the rail and hurt his head. That's what he would testify if Whitney was brought to court on a murder charge."

"The tennis racket? That, you say, he tried to attack you with?"

"His word against my word," Heimrich said. "As for the racket, it's clean, Captain. No blood on it, according to the laboratory of your hospital. Oh, a section of the gut in the groove looks as if it had been scrubbed. Abraded. Probably would have snapped under pressure. If somebody used the racket to hit a tennis ball instead of a head. But that's not enough, Captain. And—it's the only thing tangible."

186

"This address in the match folder. It could be proved to be written by Whitney?"

"It could be said to be. By one handwriting expert. It could —and I assure you in court it would—be said not to be by another expert. And both might be honest men. It isn't an exact science, you know. And the writing is brief and cramped. And even if it's proved to be Whitney's writing, murder isn't proved, Captain. All that's proved is that Whitney knew the address of a corporation in Zagreb. Probably a corporation with perfectly legitimate operations and a good credit standing. It would be, you know."

Di Scarlotti lighted a cigarette and drew on it angrily.

"It is murder," he said. "In my ship. And—and you say we can do nothing?"

"No," Heimrich said. He pushed the wireless message from a man named Parsons across the table. Di Scarlotti read it. He shook his head. He said, " 'Our dirty linen'? I do not understand. Parsons? The man you sent a message to. But—"

"Not washed in public," Heimrich said. "In other words, Her Majesty's government will handle Major Whitney, who is a British subject. And an army officer. Court-martial? Violation of the Official Secrets Act? I don't know, Captain. Both at a guess. And Parsons is coming to pick him up in Lisbon. With, I suppose, the cooperation of the Portuguese authorities. He won't get off easy. Sir Ronald had already reported on him, I think. By telephone to something called Continental Forwarding, Limited. Which is almost certainly a good deal more than that."

"It was murder in my ship," di Scarlotti said. "I am master of my ship, Inspector. I can hold this Whitney."

"Naturally," Merton Heimrich said. "You can hold him. It's up to you. But—you can't hold me, Captain. My wife and I are getting off at Málaga. It says so on our ticket."

He stood up. Comandante di Scarlotti looked up at him.

"You make things difficult, Inspector," di Scarlotti said. "Most difficult."

"Well," Heimrich said, "you've made things rather difficult for me."

Di Scarlotti sat for a moment. He reached toward the pack of cigarettes in front of him. But then, instead of taking a cigarette, he stood up. He reached a hand across the table, and Heimrich took the extended hand.

"We are still in your debt, Inspector," di Scarlotti said. Unexpectedly, he smiled. "As is Her Majesty's government," he said. "I hope they will be equally appreciative."

It was raining heavily when *Italia* tied up in Lisbon at nine on Sunday morning.

The Heimrichs had breakfast early in their cabin and looked out of portholes and Susan said, "Ugh!"

"I agree with you," Merton said. "The precise word for it. Still—it could be only a shower, of course. We could still—"

They had planned to get a taxi and be driven around Lisbon; perhaps even to have lunch in Lisbon, being sure to be back aboard before the ship sailed at two in the afternoon. They dressed for that. They went down to the foyer, which was full of people. There was a line at the purser's desk. People were collecting landing tickets and passports. The ship was tied up to starboard and doors were open onto a streaming deck—a deck which appeared submerged. Chill air came in through the open doors. On the dock, very wet men were manhandling a gangplank to the ship's side and making angry sounds to one another, presumably in Portuguese.

"Ugh," Susan said, and Heimrich said, "No, I guess not."

"All cities are alike in the rain," Susan said. "Rain is the same everywhere. We can sit on the enclosed deck and look at Lisbon through the rain. We can stay dry and warm."

Heimrich said, "Yes."

"And," Susan said, "Lisbon has never meant a great deal to me. Rome, yes, and certainly Venice and London. But not Lisbon."

There was no place to sit down. They were jostled in the crowded foyer. "We could go up—" Susan said, but did not finish because Heimrich was so intently watching the men who were making the gangplank fast to the ship.

When it was fast, there was a surge toward the doors—a surge of people who were going to see Lisbon, rain or no rain; of people at journey's end. But a ship's officer gestured them back because three men were coming up the gangplank. One of them was in uniform. A policeman's uniform, Heimrich guessed, although it was not a uniform he knew.

One of the men was a solid man in a dark suit. A formidable-looking man. He closed an umbrella when he was in the shelter of the deck's overhead. He had a hat crammed firmly on his head.

The third man was not especially solid. He wore a belted raincoat and no hat, and smooth blond hair was plastered to a rather long head. It was he who led the others into the ship. It was he who asked something of the officer at the door. The officer gestured, pointing toward an elevator. The man in the raincoat led the others toward the elevator.

A tall young man in uniform came up the gangplank. Inside the ship, he stripped off a wet raincoat. He was British army, as Heimrich had expected. He was a subaltern, with the pips of one. He looked around the crowded foyer.

Lady Ellen Grimes came from among people. They were close enough to hear her say, "Michael. Michael dear," and to see the tall young soldier, who looked rather as Sir Ronald might have looked some thirty-five years ago, put his arms around Ellen Grimes and hold her close. And then, an arm still around her shoulders, he went with her to the purser's desk and took the landing card and passport handed him.

189

"It might at least have been a sunny day for her," Susan said. "That much she had coming. Perhaps the sun will come out again in England."

Heimrich looked down at his wife, and saw that her eyes were wet, although she had not been out in the rain. He put a hand on her arm and pressed it.

"We're so lucky," Susan said, and they went to a table made of wood and knocked on it.

People streamed off the ship, down the gangplank into the rain on the pier. After a few minutes the foyer was almost empty. Susan looked up at Merton and raised enquiring eyebrows. He shook his head slightly. They waited for several minutes and then four men came from the elevator—the policeman in uniform, and the solid man who carried a furled umbrella and the hatless man with the long head and the pale smooth hair. And Major Ian Whitney, who walked behind the policeman in uniform and in front of the policeman who was not in uniform and who looked straight ahead. There was a bruise on his jaw.

The policemen and Whitney went down the gangplank to the pier. A car nudged its way along the pier, and they got into it. The man with the pale hair stopped at the door from the foyer and said something to the ship's officer stationed there. He was, Heimrich saw, the junior officer who had brought messages from Comandante Antonio di Scarlotti. The officer pointed, and the man with pale hair came across the room to them and said, "Heimrich?"

Merton Heimrich nodded his head.

"Parsons," the pale-haired man said. "Good job, if you don't mind my saying so."

"I don't mind," Heimrich said.

"The skipper isn't too happy," Parsons said. "See his point, of course. But there you are, aren't you?"

"Yes."

190

"But we're happy," Parsons said. "Quite happy, old man."
And he held out his hand, and Heimrich shook his hand.
The contact was brief.

"Can't keep them waiting, y'know," Parsons said and went
across the foyer and out to the deck and down the gangplank.
They watched him get into the car with the others. They did
not wait to see the car turn and move back along the pier.

It was dark and gray through the portholes, and the ship
was no longer vibrating. It seemed to be drifting motionless
in gray water. "Málaga?" Susan said, and Merton Heimrich
said, "I'm afraid so, dear."

Angela and Guido brought them breakfast, and Heimrich
gave them money. (Too much? Or did they always beam so?)

"You were good to us," Susan said.

Angela said, "It was a pleasure, signora," as if she meant
it, and Guido said, "Indeed, signor-signora."

And men came into the cabin and carried luggage out of it.

At the foot of the gangplank, when the Heimrichs had
walked down it, a man stood with a square of cardboard held
above his head. A word was hand-lettered on the cardboard.
The word was "Heimlich."

"Close enough," Heimrich said. "Probably our man."

It was their man—the man arranged for by distant Miss
Snell to drive them from Málaga to Nerja. It took half an
hour to retrieve their luggage and to clear it through customs.
But the customs man asked only that one small bag be
opened and scrawled indecipherable letters on the others.

The sun came out as they left the busy streets of Málaga.
They went along a narrow road which twisted around out-
croppings of rock. Sometimes they could see the Mediterranean. On the other side, they could sometimes see high
mountains with snow on their tops. Always they could see
mules, heavy-laden, resigned, led by men who looked as if

they had always led resigned mules. They edged around the mules; they cringed away from trucks headed for Málaga. They went through small towns.

High-rise apartment buildings, some finished, some partly built, climbed the hills to the left as they went east along the coast toward Nerja. Now and then there were angular structures between the road and the sea.

"It's trying to be Miami Beach," Susan said. "That Miss Snell. Unspoiled fishing villages."

He looked at her with anxiety. But her smile was her own smile, and her eyes were bright again, and she put a hand on one of his and left it there.

The buildings were less frequent as they drove on through the sunshine; more often they could see the Mediterranean sparkling under the sun. Nerja was small, and small streets squiggled from a central square.

The *parador* was beyond the center of the town, but not much beyond it. It was on a cliff above the sea, and their room, on the third floor, had a balcony on the ocean side, and the sun was bright on the balcony. Heimrich had got pesetas for traveler's checks before they left the ship, and he tipped the boy who had brought up their bags and, although he already knew pesetas were going to be hard to get used to, apparently tipped him enough. The boy made approving sounds in Spanish and went out of the room.

They went out onto the balcony and into the sun. Far below there was a beach, and nets were drying on it, and one of the nets was being mended by two men. The sun was very bright.

"Holiday," Susan Heimrich said. "We're on holiday, dear."

Heimrich said, "Yes, Susan."

"But in a way," Susan said, "we take it with us, no matter what."

Heimrich looked at her carefully. She looked fine. He said, "Yes, Susan. No matter what. You bring it with us."